FATE

OF THE

WATCHMAN

FATE
OF THE
WATCHMAN

CHAD PETTIT

JOURNEY OF FATE - BOOK ONE

Ambassador International
GREENVILLE, SOUTH CAROLINA & BELFAST, NORTHERN IRELAND

www.ambassador-international.com

Fate of the Watchman

ISBN: 978-1-93550-770-3

eISBN: 978-1-62020-915-8

This is a work of fiction. Names, characters, and incidents are all products of the author's imagination or are used for fictional purposes. Any resemblance to actual events or persons, living or dead, is entirely coincidental. Any mentioned brand names, places, and trademarks remain the property of their respective owners, bear no association with the author or the publisher, and are used for fictional purposes only.

Scripture taken from the King James Version, The Authorized Version. Public Domain.

Cover Design & Typesetting by Hannah Nichols
Ebook Conversion by Anna Riebe Raats
Edited by Katie Cruice Smith

AMBASSADOR INTERNATIONAL
Emerald House
411 University Ridge, Suite B14
Greenville, SC 29601, USA
www.ambassador-international.com

AMBASSADOR BOOKS
The Mount
2 Woodstock Link
Belfast, BT6 8DD, Northern Ireland, UK
www.ambassadormedia.co.uk

The colophon is a trademark of Ambassador, a Christian publishing company.

Chapter 1

THE TEST OF HELP

SOME PATHS ARE FORGED. SOME paths are simply laid. But all paths are created. Many trails have been stamped out over time as men have trodden over lands, while others have been cut out by the machinations of civilizations as they grow and change. Often though, there is no clear path that lies between the beginning and the end; it is simply the name given to the journey along the way to the destination, which may or may not be physical and seen. Everyone walks many paths to many destinations—those paths intersecting and breaking, meeting and intertwining—though often unnoticed.

Standing perfectly still behind the tall desk of his automotive shop, Lester Sharp was walking one of those paths, one about to be intersected. He stood beneath bright, fluorescent white lights, sorting through an inch-high stack of reports marked with countless lines of names and numbers that seemed to bleed together. Intermittently, he glanced at the screen of the constantly buzzing phone in his hand, navigating through equally blurring emails and text messages. His trance was nearly so perfect that the coughing on the other side of the counter was almost not enough to pull him from the spell of occupational drudgery.

"Dave! Customer," Lester said without looking away from his papers.

A distant, almost muffled shout of "pulling a part, be there'n a minute" forced an agitated sigh from Lester. He looked up, reminding himself to put on the sincerest version of his manufactured smile, and spoke before his eyes had cleared the counter.

"Sorry about that. What can I do . . ." His question trailed off when he looked over the counter and saw a dark-skinned, slender man in his early twenties with long dreadlocks and warm, blue eyes.

"For you," the young man said.

Lester blinked and scrunched up his face. "What?"

"For you," the man said with a slight shrug. "You were trying to say: What can I do for you? Right?"

"Right," Lester said gruffly, setting his phone on the counter. "Sorry about that. Whatcha need?"

The man stepped back and shoved his hands into his pockets. Looking at the ground, he replied. "I hate to even ask, sir, but I could really use some help."

Lester furrowed his eyebrows. "Well, that's what we're here for. You need parts, or do you need us to fix something up for you?"

The man looked up and took a deep breath. "Nah, it's not my car, man. I'm just really hungry."

Lester frowned. He noticed how skinny the man was then, saw that his face and hands were dry and his skin cracked. "Can't help you, man." He looked back to his stack of papers. "There's a couple restaurants around the corner."

"I don't exactly have any money, sir. I was hoping you could maybe lend me a few bucks."

Lester slammed his fist onto the stack of papers and looked up again. "Look, I said I can't help you. Try the shelter."

The man pulled his hands from his pockets and put them together at his waist. "Please. Just a little help."

Lester shook his head. "Why don't you try helping yourself, huh?"

The man smiled and held up his hand, pointing. "Oh, I get it. You think everybody that asks for money just doesn't want to try. That it?"

Lester saw his heavy-set manager, Dave, coming from the back out of the corner of his eye. "Dave, get this guy out of here."

"What's the problem?" Dave asked as he set his chubby hand on the counter.

"Another one asking for a handout," Lester said.

"One?" The man interrupted. "Wow."

Lester rolled his eyes. "Oh, that's not what I meant."

"Nah, clearly. I mean, you almost passed out when you saw who it was in front of your counter, and you just assume anyone like me needs a hand out." The skinny man leaned his head back.

Lester breathed so sharply through his nose that it almost whistled. "Like I said, it's not like that. I just don't give handouts. You want something to eat? Get a job." He looked at Dave and nodded toward the door. Dave looked back grimly and nodded after a moment.

The man held a hand up, palm facing Lester. "Nah, man. You ain't gotta throw me out." He pointed to the wall behind Lester. "Nice decoration. Guess that's all it is, though."

Lester looked up and over his shoulder to the wall behind him. The bold words painted on the wall almost surprised him. He had nearly forgotten that he had painted them there years ago. He paused long enough to read the quote from the Bible: *I have set watchmen upon thy walls, O Jerusalem, which shall never hold their peace day nor night: ye that make mention of the LORD, keep not silence.*

The bell above the glass door to the front of the shop chimed, pulling Lester's eyes away from the wall. He turned and looked at the skinny stranger inside the door, holding it with one hand.

"Be seeing you, Lester," he said as he pointed. Then he stepped all the way out of the shop and let the door swing shut.

"Whatcha think he meant by that?" Dave asked.

Lester turned to look at him. "Means he'll be back to ask for more money." He shrugged. "What else?"

Dave looked around. "Got a bad feeling about it, Les."

"Yeah?" Lester poked his bottom lip out and rocked his head back and forth. "Well, I don't pay you for your feelings. I pay you to keep this place running and get all of these records in order." He held up the stack of papers for Dave to see. "And what it looks like is I'm not getting my money's worth."

"How can I fix the files if you're always looking through them?" Dave asked. "And why'd you kick that guy out?"

Lester set the papers on the counter. "Kick him out? Did you not just see him walk out on his own?"

"I sure did, right after you told me to get him outta here." Lester paused to look at his manager carefully. He was almost never that bold. He would usually take whatever task list or orders Lester gave him and never complained or confronted Lester about anything.

"What's gotten into you?" He asked as he sat on the edge of the counter.

Dave shook his head. "Nothing."

"Nothing?" Lester asked.

"Nothing."

"Look," Lester said with a shake of his head. "You give somebody a few bucks here, a few bucks there—seems innocent enough, right? Seems like the right thing to do. Right up until when they're coming around every day with their hand out. Once you start down that road, there's no turning back."

Dave laughed. "How would you know? I don't think we could pull a donation out of you with a forklift."

"Ha ha," Lester said. "Anyway, it's late. I'm going home to finish up. I just need you to email me projections for next month on new and used parts sales before you get outta here."

Dave groaned.

"What?"

Dave took a deep breath. "Like you said: it's late. Can't it wait 'til tomorrow, Les?"

"Hey, I'll be up late working way past when you finish up here. It's not like I'm asking you to do something I wouldn't do myself." He slipped his phone into his pocket and then walked over and put a hand on Dave's shoulder. "Right?"

Dave nodded.

Lester patted him on the shoulder. "Atta boy. Sooner you get it done, the sooner you get to go home."

"Not like it matters," Dave said under his breath.

"What?" Lester asked as he reached for his jacket.

"Nothing."

Lester eyed Dave for a few moments, but then he decided to let it go. "Alright. See you in the morning, Dave."

"Night, Les."

Lester left the shop with the papers he had been looking at in a folder under his arm and walked quickly to his car, an immaculate, black sedan with tinted windows. He pulled the driver's side door open and got in awkwardly, holding the folder of papers in one hand and a few resumés in the other. He tossed it all into the passenger's seat as he dropped into the driver's seat. When the door was shut, he took a deep breath before pressing his foot on the brake and tapping the start button.

He put the car in gear once the engine hummed to life and pulled off with a jerky burst of acceleration. He weaved in and out of the slower cars on the crowded street, ignoring the dirty looks and hand gestures those he had cut off gave him and even laughing a few times. He was not sure why he was in such a rush. He was going home to do the same amount of work he was doing at the shop, but he liked the feeling of being ahead of everyone else, being in control. The speed felt good, and he pressed the pedal closer to the floorboard when he had gone through the last yellow light of the main part of town.

Lester stopped in front of his mailbox at the end of his driveway, trying his best not to notice the overgrown lawn leading up to his small, brick house. He shoved the gear shift into park and leaned back in his seat. The fence at the sides of the house he and his brother Dillon had put up three years prior was leaning in several places, and the graying of the stained cedar was obvious, even in the crystalline light of the half-moon. He shook his head and unbuckled his seatbelt, then climbed painfully out of the car with a groan.

There was a thick stack of mail in the box, which gave Lester a sense of dread and hope in the same flutter of his anxious heart. He could see the bills right away by the white, rectangular envelopes with their smaller, clear plastic rectangles that covered his own address in the middle. As he pulled the stack out, he saw several of the bills, credit card offers, and a large, white envelope marked *Voice of the Martyrs*. He tried his best not to look at the picture of the Somalian woman weeping on the front of the envelope as he reshuffled it to the bottom of the stack. The thought of it was quickly replaced by his name on another envelope in familiar handwriting. He looked up in the top left corner of the envelope and saw the name and rank: SSG Dillon Sharp, along with the IPO address he had memorized.

Lester smiled a rare but fleeting smile on the way back to his car.

Chapter 2

THE HANDS ON THE CLOCK

IN ALL THE WORLD, THERE is not a more truthful liar than a clock. The myriad hands tick away on walls, wrists, appliances, and punch clocks with the consistent, persistent promise of another second, another minute, another hour. Its faithful worshippers bow to it day and night, groaning their praises from pillows to coffee makers, from traffic jams to cubicles to warehouses. Some pray to it, begging it to stretch or shrink, and it stares back into their bloodshot eyes with feigned compassion, pretending to rush, pretending to last forever.

So it was for Lester as he sat alone in his home office, leaning back in his creaking swivel chair, his sleepy gaze obediently following the thin second hand as it ticked its way around the black and white face of the wall clock above his disheveled desk. Five minutes until midnight. With a creak and a groan, he came forward, bracing himself with his hands against the false wooden frame of the desktop to compensate for the sudden rush of movement. He rubbed his eyes for the fortieth time before reaching back down to the random piles of sticky notes, deposit slips, tax forms, schedules, and the seemingly bottomless stack of resumés he'd pushed to his far right.

In his mind's eye, he was still monitoring the relentless ticking of the second hand, made worse by the insistent sound it made as it forced its way around once more. Four minutes until midnight. Five hours and four minutes until he had to wake up. With his head and neck bent over the barely legible calendar filled with notes, stains, and what seemed like a hundred scratched out and cancelled meetings, he lifted his eyes to glance at the blue mug he knew was an eighth filled with lukewarm Columbian roast residue. He felt his shoulders lift and fall heavily and sluggishly as he suddenly took an unnatural portion of stale air in through his nose and then hissed it out through pursed lips.

That brief glance in the direction of the mug took his half-opened gaze unavoidably to the right of the coffee cup, where a picture frame leaned, nearly buried beneath the multiple-page report from an OSHA inspector and the contractor quotes prompted by that report. Allowing himself a moment to view the recent photo that was crookedly placed into the frame, he saw a somewhat fresher version of himself with his short, black hair actually combed back and a smile on his face, right arm around the back of his brother, Dillon, who was wearing an army combat uniform with matching hat and black Oakley sunglasses. Dillon's smile was bigger than Lester's; so was Dillon's body, obviously well-muscled, even in the loose-fitting uniform.

Lester sighed slowly, leaned his head back, and looked up at the clock. Three minutes to midnight. His body ached in response, his muscles and bones calling out for him to sleep. He ignored those sensations, scooping up his smartphone with his right hand. He hit the button on the right side that would light up the screen and then adjusted the phone in his hand so that he could use the same thumb to swipe the pattern that unlocked the device. Before the screen was even fully switched, he was tapping where he knew the email icon was. His email was full of highlighted, unread messages from employees, the bank, inspectors, contractors, and various family members. Not seeing a message from Dave, he tossed the phone onto the desk, where it tried to bounce but simply thudded onto the pressboard surface.

Two minutes to midnight. He sighed and closed his eyes, trying to remember what he needed to discuss in the morning meeting so that he could scribble it into the notes he had made on a half-torn sheet of paper beside the calendar in front of him. No use. His mind was so full that it was blank. He opened his eyes with a start, throwing his hands out wide to brace himself from falling. It took him a moment to realize that he was still sitting perfectly still in his chair. He took a deep breath and shook his head, wondering how he could fall asleep that quickly.

One minute to midnight. Staring at the clock, Lester let out a sound that was somewhere between a confused grunt and a snort, amazed by the fact that he had closed his eyes for only a second, and yet a minute had gone by. With a loud creak, he rose from the swivel chair, simultaneously swiping his coffee cup from the desk in his left hand. The seat of the chair brushed against the back of his legs annoyingly as he stood, hindering him from moving away from the desk, so he growled and thrust his right leg back. The movement across carpet was mainly in vain; the stubborn chair moved back barely an inch. He growled again and turned, reaching down to the arm of the chair as he did, so that he could push it back. The sudden movement caused the lukewarm coffee to slosh around in the bottom of the cup so violently that a few drops flew over the rim of the mug and splashed onto the floor, one or two of them soaking into his arm.

He lifted his head and groaned, then waved his hand in silent surrender and walked out of the office. The door was open, but he still pushed on it as he exited, and the force caused the bottom of it to push against the spring door-stopper against the wall. The door bounced back and hit his shoulder, causing another frustrated groan to escape him as he stomped down the hall. He grumbled as he walked, mumbling to himself about the manager that he had hired to do all of the things he was doing now, complaining about having to wake up in a few hours yet still being up.

The hallway was short, and he arrived in the kitchen, which opened to the left, in a few seconds. As he turned the corner and started walking toward the counter where the coffeemaker sat waiting, he saw the time displayed on it in glowing green numbers. As soon as he reached it, the time switched to midnight. That did little to boost his morale, but he was too caught up in his incoherent monologue to even bother letting out another groan. He yanked the pot from the warmer and slapped the pour spout onto the lip of his mug, nearly cracking both, then jerked the pot up to a nearly inverted position to get the last of the burnt liquid into the cup. After banging the carafe against the inside of the now half-empty mug unceremoniously, he shoved it back onto the warmer and then turned around so that he could lean against the counter.

He was still grumbling as he slowly lifted the mug to his lips but then paused and let out a long breath that seemed to freeze all of his thoughts and emotions. He felt the warmth of the mug and the steam of the coffee against his face, and it calmed him momentarily. The kitchen was quiet, his exhale frozen on the air. He almost hated to take a drink, afraid the slurping would break the temporary spell that had instantly emptied him of anger because he knew the first sip would end the enchantment. The sip came, but the spell remained. The slurp echoed in his mind, reverberating off the kitchen cabinets, but the silence was still present. The meeting disappeared into the next sip, dissolved into the bitter black liquid as it cascaded over his teeth and trickled its way over his tongue to his throat.

Everything was still and hushed.

Bewitched by the magic of the drink, Lester continued to lean against the counter for what seemed like an eternity—methodically, patiently taking sip after sip, not even noticing the burned taste of the coffee as it burned his tongue. He was mesmerized by the silence, which hung in the air thickly as if a blanket of quiet had been strung from one end of the kitchen to the other, and he was lost in its folds.

But then it was no longer magic. It was odd. It was wrong.

Lester slowly lowered the cup to his waist and pushed himself off the counter. Curiosity and trepidation crept into his mind as he slowly turned around. His eyes immediately went to the clock display on the coffeemaker. He could tell that something was out of place before he had turned all the way around, and what he saw only confirmed his fears.

Midnight.

The display hadn't changed. He wasn't sure what to make of that at first, but Lester found himself setting the cup on the counter slowly, never taking his eyes off the timer. He thought that he had been sipping his coffee for at least a minute, more likely two, but the time was still midnight. He glanced down and saw that the cup was nearly empty again. There was no way that he had drunk even half of it in less than a minute. He put both hands against the counter and looked up and to his right. Both the clock on the stove and the one on the microwave above it displayed the same time.

Midnight.

Lester stood up straight, clearing his throat, and brought his left arm up so that he could read his wristwatch. A gift from his brother the day he had left for Iraq, the watch was made of gold with a dark leather band, and the face was a light gold color with finely crafted hands that circled it with precision and grace. He pressed his lips together and swallowed hard when he saw the second hand frozen in place. Although the watch had tiny adjustment knobs on the side, it was not the kind of watch that a person had to wind up every day, and it was only six months old. He opened his mouth and took a deep breath, letting his arm slip back to his side. He shook his head and then waved both hands helplessly before stepping out of the kitchen, back into the hallway, toward the office.

He wasted no time speeding down the hallway as fast as his heavy legs would carry him and stepping through the office door. His head was turned to the wall behind his desk before he even made it through the doorway, so he saw the clock on the wall stuck at midnight before he had made it all the way into the office. He stood still for several moments, shaking his head slowly from left to right. Taking another deep breath to steady himself, he finally walked up to the desk, pulled the clock down, and yanked the battery out of the back. He used one of the few extra batteries he kept in the drawer of the desk to replace the battery and then hurriedly flipped the clock over in his arms to listen and look for the ticking of the second hand.

Nothing.

Not even looking down, Lester set the clock on the desk on top of papers he was no longer paying attention to or thinking about. He had heard of people hallucinating from lack of sleep but never thought that he would get to that point. Still, he reasoned, the only possible explanation for all of the clocks being frozen was a hallucination of his subconscious mind telling him that he desperately needed rest. Lester took the hint and walked out of the office. This time, once in the hallway, he turned to the left. His bedroom was perpendicular to the hallway so that the walls of his bedroom were partly joined with the office and partly joined with the living room that was between his office and the kitchen. He opened the door and took a straight line to the large, queen-size bed that was messy from the day before and flopped unceremoniously onto it, still fully dressed. As he rolled to his right shoulder, he saw the red display of the the alarm clock.

Midnight.

He groaned and buried his head in his pillow. Sleep. He just needed sleep.

Chapter 3

WAKING UP

The moment between asleep and awake is a deceitful glitch in the mechanism of the mind. Less than a split second of time between consciousness and unconsciousness, it is really an eternity of resolved and unresolved choices, ensconced guilt, and elusive secrets dangled before the unseeing eyes of finite men and women. In that lightning quick snap of the ethereal fingers of time exists a thousand deaths, a thousand lives, and the endless rain of memory. It pours out on the helpless souls that come to its door seeking solace, only to be cruelly tortured by glimpses of what could but never will be or distorted collages of a person's greatest fears before being thrust away into the waking world. Before the moment has completed its game of dread, it gives its victims the kiss of confusion so that the return to the world of the waking is accompanied by the unclear, partially concealed, and haunting images of a false reality.

Lester found himself in that place of torture, frozen on a sea of hands that seemed so familiar, so strange, all at once supporting him, yet letting him fall. He groped for the exit—a giant clock with the second hand twisted into a pull handle—inches from his outstretched arms, but the waves beneath him grabbed and pulled at him, dragging him away, pushing him closer, repeating. The sky was made up of a million darkened mouths opened and screaming, sending their screeching cries like some abstract thunder that grated on his sensitive ears. The screams from above, the shouts from below—all of it seemed to drown in a sea of his own agonized pleas for help, for mercy. None came; and after his last attempt at reaching the door in an eternity of useless attempts failed, the door twisted back into the normal shape of the clock.

The sky cleared to reddish black. The hands became a raft floating upon a crimson sea. The clock hung on nothing. Lester saw its sadistic hands locked at twelve, and he buried his face in his hands, hands that once again had been covered in the blood of the sea beneath and around him. He knew his torture would never end as the sea turned to hands, and the sky began to distort into a sea of mouths. The door began to stretch and twist, the mocking hands never moving.

Lester sat up in his bed, slipping for a moment in his own sweat but managing to grip the sheets, the real sheets. Simultaneously warm and cold. Tangible. He let out a relieved sigh and loosened his grip on those temporary anchors to reality, allowing his body to relax. The light of the moon coming through a slit in the bedroom curtains made his forearm glisten silvery-blue as he brought it to his cheek to wipe away the salty tears that had drifted from his puffy eyes. Salt mixed with salt, uncomfortable moisture with moisture, as anxiety and anguish collided.

Only a dream.

The lie sounded good to him, soothing, consoling. He turned to his right to regard the alarm clock on the nightstand beside the bed and exposed the lie for the false hope that it was. The red LED display was clear and bright in the dark room with no chance for any other possibility.

Midnight.

Lester could barely draw breath. How could this be? His mind raced through a maze of possible rationales but returned to the starting line empty-handed. Just the clock. He unconvincingly told himself that it was just this clock. All of this was coincidence, eerily so, but coincidence, nonetheless. He threw the covers up and away from his body and swung his legs over the edge of the bed. He was on his feet and moving toward the door before he could think about it. Then he was in the hallway, practically running toward the faint blue glow seeping into the hallway from the kitchen.

As he rounded the corner and came into the kitchen, he grabbed the wall with his left hand to keep from sliding and falling, but he never let himself slow down. He stalked up to the stove, his eyes unblinking, as if to intimidate the clock over the stove to change from the unyielding numbers displayed there.

12:00

His determined stride became a lead-footed, shoulder-drooped slide as he closed the remainder of the distance to the stove and then leaned on the counter next to it with his hands out in front of him. The edges of the laminate countertop practically cut into the palms of his hands because he was putting so much of his exhausted weight on it, but he hardly noticed. He took several deep breaths before lifting his eyes up to scan the dimly lit numbers on the coffeemaker; then he shook his head slowly back and forth when the numbers confirmed what he already knew.

Trapped in a dream. That was it. Lester laughed at himself as the truth became apparent.

"You have got to get some sleep, man." He paused after speaking to himself when he noticed an echo from the words. It was oddly hollow and out of place. It was not the sort of echo that comes from a voice bouncing off the walls of a large room or cave. This sounded like he was in some isolated place where the sound could not escape. In fact, he realized, everything was entirely too still. There was no buzzing sound from the refrigerator. There was no humming of the fans in the other room. It was as silent as a grave, as if death had come in the night and shrouded the house in its dark cloak.

Lester blinked several times, trying to clear the exhaustion and partial sleep. He looked next to the coffeemaker and saw the mug he had left there before going to bed. It registered, as if on cue, that this was all induced by sleep deprivation, fueled by too much caffeine. With a sigh, Lester stood up and moved to where the mug was. Thinking that the contents of the half-empty cup would be room temperature by that point, he didn't bother grabbing the handle; but as his hand wrapped around the sides of the mug, he felt a sharp and sudden burning sensation. He snatched his hand away quickly, reeling it all the way back to his face, shaking the fingers.

That's when he noticed that there was a line of steam running from the inside of the mug to the ceiling. Although he could not see the steam all the way to the ceiling, the thin, ghostly material was fully visible at the lip of the mug. He leaned in closer, drawn in by something peculiar, something almost sinister. When the truth became clear, Lester gasped and jumped back.

The steam was not rising. It was not moving at all.

Cautiously, he leaned back in and studied the vapor that was frozen in its climb into nothingness. He shifted his gaze several times from the steam to the clock on the coffeemaker. Frozen. He tried with all of his mental faculties to deny the obvious conclusion, but he was left with no meat to his argument.

Time had stopped.

Lester turned and ran out of the kitchen, down the hall, and into his bedroom. He came in to the bed so quickly that his legs slammed into the side of it and lurched his body forward. After righting himself, he grabbed the cell phone from the nightstand and hurriedly pressed the side button to light up the screen. After swiping in the passcode, he hit the call icon immediately and called Dave. He knew that it was insane to call someone at this hour, but he also knew that the only person in his life that would answer the phone would be Dave.

When the phone had been to his ear for several seconds without ringing, he paused. His mind caught up to his actions a moment later. He realized that when he had tried to unlock the screen, nothing had happened. In fact, the screen never even registered that his finger had swiped across the series of dots because the screen was frozen. He slowly lowered the phone and brought it in front of his face. Sure enough, it was frozen. Black. He took a deep breath and closed his eyes. Going through the procedure of calling his general manager had become so routine and habitual that he could not even realize that he was doing it all on muscle memory without actually doing anything. After several attempts to get the screen to light up, he growled and threw it on the bed. He stormed out of the bedroom and stomped across the house to the front door, grabbed his keys off the rack mounted to the wall, slid his feet into a pair of worn out slides, and went outside.

As soon as he walked onto his wooden steps, he realized that he was now outside in a pair of boxer shorts and a stretched-out tank top. Better judgment led him back to the bedroom, where he hurriedly slipped on a plain white t-shirt, faded jeans, and an old pair of gray running shoes before rushing back out the front door. He stomped down the short sidewalk, past the edge of the house, and up to his crookedly parked car. He grabbed the driver side door handle and jerked the door open. There was a chirping sound as the vehicle registered the key fob in his hand. He flopped unceremoniously into the leather driver's seat and yanked the door shut beside him. He quickly tossed the keys into the empty passenger's seat and then started the car with a frustrated growl.

The small but powerful engine came to life with a roar that expressed Lester's grateful elation. Something was working. He just had to get out of his house. Now he would drive through town, see everything normal, and come home with a fresh pair of eyes and his mind cleared of some of the clutter.

Clutter. That word struck a nerve with Lester as he backed out of his driveway onto the crowded street. He lived in the most typical neighborhood there was. Every house the same, every family different, yet exactly alike. Every house was either odd or even with the identical kitchen to the left or the right, depending on which side of the street it had been built. Single family homes with multiple cars overflowing from the concrete driveways to the partially trimmed curbside. Red, white, and black. Cars were never blue and silver anymore. A sprinkling of off-road pickup trucks with balding street tires jutted out too far from curbs, making the street dangerously narrow for one car, let alone the never-ending stream of people taking shortcuts to work and the next-door neighbors, always in a rush, never speaking, always going opposite directions.

Lester tried to suppress a growl through clenched teeth as he manipulated his way down the street, past the cars, past the green trash cans against the edges of the ant pile-ridden curbs. Lights were out in all of the houses, but many people kept their security lights on, which cast too many shadows for thieves and bored teenagers to ignore most nights. Lester thought about the latest complaints on social media about the newest rash of break-ins and doors or lawns that had been the victims of egg and toilet paper violence as he approached the edge of the street. No point worrying about it now, he told himself.

But then something curious caught his attention. Nearing the half-bent-over stop sign at the end of his street, Lester saw lights on in the last house on the right side of the block. This was a rare home with only one small pickup in the driveway. It was silver and parked halfway onto the driveway with the bed of the truck hanging over the sidewalk. Lights on didn't mean much; but as Lester looked closer, he saw that the front door was open. Moreover, when he looked into the doorway, he saw someone lying on the floor. He tried to ignore what he had seen, but something nagged at his senses, something strong, something strangely familiar. He looked away, back to the stop sign and the cross street just beyond it.

Empty. Silent.

This scene was not natural, and Lester could feel it. Barely conscious of the action, he pushed the gear lever into the park position and lifted his foot from the brake pedal. He found himself contemplating running into the house to check on the man. He knew it was a man because he had only ever seen a man in that house. In fact, he had met him once when a package for Lester had been erroneously delivered to that address. They had met when the man had returned the package and exchanged the same obligatory small talk that all suburban Americans are required to exchange in such undesired meetings: "How are you?" That was always followed with, "Good, how are you?" To break the awkward silence, one part would volunteer to ask how long the other person had been in the neighborhood or what it was that he or she did for a living, and the inquired party would offer too much or not enough about the unsatisfying life that was more uncomfortable to discuss than to bother living.

Lester imagined and dreaded that conversation happening again and groaned, then groaned louder when he realized that the man was probably dealing with some deep personal problems and would likely want to tell someone all about it. Lester simply did not have time to hear it, nor did he care to listen. Still, his eyes could not avoid the leg lying in the living room beyond the doorway that was no doubt attached to the man's unconscious body lying out of his sight. And there was certainly no missing the trash on the lawn, the sidewalk, and into the house. Beer cans. Bottles. It was too dark to tell, but Lester assumed there was a trail of discarded cigarette butts as well.

He sighed and hit the button to shut the engine off. With a jerk, he pulled the door handle and shoved the door open. He angrily pulled himself out of the car and slammed the door shut behind him. Covering the distance from the car to the door, he did his best to put on a concerned face that would mask the irritated face enough to be seen as genuine. He made it to the doorway in a few seconds and stopped. He knocked on the half-open door softly and said hello in the friendliest, non-sociopathic voice he could muster.

How did one sound concerned and well-intentioned when intruding a strange house in the middle of the night?

There was no answer. The man didn't move. Lester could see more of both legs now, but his torso lay just beyond the hallway, in the living room. He knocked and called again, but there was no response, so Lester entered the house cautiously. "Hello?" He weaved around a few scattered beer cans as he made his way through the foyer. "I saw your light on and noticed your door was open. I'm your neighbor down the street. Lester. We met last year?"

Silence.

Lester finally stepped onto the dingy carpet of the living room, and his shoulders drooped at the sight. The man was face-down on the floor with his arms sprawled out awkwardly. Surrounding the man were numerous empty beer cans, an empty liquor bottle, and a half-empty pill bottle. Lester felt his heart beating faster, but he approached the man anyway. Something—that same feeling—nagged at him. As he knelt down next to him, he knew that the man was dead. He didn't need to, but he pulled the man over and checked his pulse.

Nothing.

He checked his breathing.

Nothing.

The man's face was locked in an expression of horror, his lips beginning to turn blue and his eyes glazed over. Lester let out a long sigh and then sat back on his legs. He stayed that way for nearly a minute. He had never seen a dead body before, not even at funerals because no one did those open caskets anymore. He glanced up and saw a cell phone on the gray couch in front of him. Remembering that he had left his own phone on his bed, Lester reached out and grabbed it. The screen was lit up without need for a password. He tried not to notice the background of the man with a woman and young boy that Lester had never seen him with. He tried not to notice the man's smile, so much different than the scowl Lester always received when driving past this house. He tried not to notice the man's ring on his left hand as he looked away. He tried.

He touched the call icon with his thumb, but nothing happened. He pressed it several times with no results, so he finally hit the side button to black the screen out, but nothing came from that effort either. It took another moment for him to read the numbers on the digital clock display of the phone.

12:00.

He stood and then threw the phone at the couch. It bounced into the cushions and onto the floor next to the man. His heart racing, Lester fell to his knees and grabbed the man's head with both hands. He frantically went through a series of breaths, thrusts to the man's chest, doing what he hoped was CPR. The lessons from the YMCA as a teenager were drowned in years of comfort, indifference, the moment of panic, and the revulsion of putting his mouth on the mouth of another man. This man—this man he didn't really know, pretended he hadn't met—the man lying dead beneath his interlocked, thrusting hands. Again, he checked for breathing, heard only his own. He screamed with all of the power he could pull from primal roots that threatened to be yanked out through strained vocal cords.

Silence. Death.

With a growl, Lester rose. He stood over the man and let out a resigned sigh. He shook his head, pressed his lips together, and breathed heavily out of his nose. Realizing there was nothing more he could do, he stomped out of the house. Driving all the way to the police station to report a death in the middle of the night was not high on his priority list, but he had no choice. There was no way that he could leave the man that way without reporting it. No one—not even this depraved drunk—deserved to die and be left this way. His world upside down and mind inside out, Lester stormed toward the door. His head was down as he walked through the doorway, so he didn't know where the voice that spoke to him in the next moment came from.

"Hey, man, you going to the police?"

Lester stopped and gasped, lifted his head, and jumped back. He clutched his chest with his right hand and slapped his left hand against the bricks on the side of the house to brace himself. The sound of a man's voice had scared him beyond anything that he could remember; but when he looked up and saw the same man that had come into his shop looking for money for food leaning against his car, Lester was terrified.

He half-screamed, half-gasped. "Who are you, and where did you come from?"

The stranger stopped him with a raised hand. "Does it really matter?"

Lester stood up straight, chest heaving and eyes wide as he tried to take it in, tried to breathe in the scene, this man, and this night. Panic came out of his mouth like vapor in the form of shaking, short breaths. He closed his mouth, swallowed, licked his lips, opened his mouth again, and let the fear escape. Finally mustering up enough courage, he addressed the stranger with a firm voice.

"What are you doing here?"

The stranger laughed. "Told you I'd be seeing you, man."

Lester took a step back. "Did you follow me?"

The stranger stood up straight and put his hands in the pockets of his jeans. "Nah. I already knew where you live. I've been watching you for a while."

Lester gasped. "What?"

The stranger nodded. "Yeah, you and everybody on this street. It's kinda my thing."

Lester forced himself to stand up straight and speak with authority. "So, you've been casing us, huh?" He nodded. "Oh, I'll be telling the police all about you."

The stranger laughed. "Come on, Lester. You don't know anything about me." He shook his head. "I don't think you're gonna be telling anybody anything."

Lester took a bold step forward and pointed at the man. "Is that a threat?"

The stranger held up a hand. "Chill, man. You got this whole thing wrong."

"Do I?"

The stranger nodded in reply. Lester paused and turned halfway around so that he could look into the house again. A terrifying thought ran through his mind, and he immediately turned back around, suddenly worried about having his back to the man.

"You killed that man, didn't you?" Lester pointed again and shook his finger. "That's why you're out here at midnight. You killed that man, so you could rob him."

"Wow." The stranger rolled his eyes. He shook his head and pointed toward the house. "Yeah, man, cause the guy is clearly loaded. I mean, all I gotta do is take his old school T.V. with the tin foil rabbit ears, the barely working pay-as-you-go phone, and the four ketchup packets he's got in his fridge, and I'll be set for life."

Lester nodded and narrowed his eyes. "Exactly. You know what he's got inside his house. This is too simple. You need money. A man's dead, and you're outside his house."

"I never actually said I needed money, man." The stranger slid his other hand back into his pocket.

That gave Lester pause, but he continued. "Admit it. You killed that man."

The strange man squeezed his eyes halfway shut and touched an index finger to his chest. He took a deep breath in for a second that stretched into three and then let it out through thin nostrils so that it shushed out like an angry person at a movie where everyone talks during the climax.

"You're asking if I killed the man in the house you just came out of?" The stranger let his hand creep back to his side and started walking forward slowly. "The man that clearly overdosed on pills and alcohol? You want to know if I killed him?" The stranger took a couple of steps toward Lester. "I get it. Black man, dark clothes, in the middle of the night. Body." He paused and nodded his head. "Yeah, I could see where you got that."

Shaking on the inside but outwardly firm as stone, Lester responded angrily. "Uh, uh. Don't you try to play that card. I don't know you; but what I do know is that this man is dead, and you just happen to be standing outside his house."

The stranger paused, shook his head, and sighed. He nodded and laughed, more snort and huff than chuckle, and his shoulders slumped. Chewing his bottom lip now, he looked at the ground for a moment.

"Was I outside the house before you went in, Lester?"

Lester wasted no time in response. "I was in a hurry. You could have been hiding around the corner. There's not much light, but plenty of shadows."

The stranger stood motionless, waiting, with a knowing smile.

The question blurted its way out of Lester's mouth. "How do you know—"

"Your name?" The stranger nodded. He stepped forward, hands in his pockets, head tilted slightly back.

"Stay away from me." Lester took a step back but thought about the way he was going and stopped. He turned his head to look back through the doorway. He saw the dead man's leg, saw the lights shining; and he remembered quickly that a strange man was approaching him. He snapped his head around and saw only darkness, the driveway, and his car on the road, still running. Terrified and wondering where the stranger had gone so quickly, he looked left and right multiple times until a voice behind him nearly sent him sprinting down the driveway. Instead, he turned and yelled all at once to face the doorway, coming face to face with the stranger.

"Yeah, I know your name. I know your phone's dead, too, and I know why, man."

Lester leaned back and nearly whimpered. "Oh, no! Am I dead?"

The stranger stepped back. "You're asking me?" A hand came out of his pocket and pointed at Lester. "Do you feel dead?"

Now it was Lester's turn to screw up his face. "No. I don't know." He paused, chewing his lip momentarily. "How does a dead person feel?"

The stranger shrugged. "Never been dead."

"What?"

"I can't tell you how a dead person feels because I've never been dead."

Lester squinted his eyes and shook his head. "Are you for real. I mean, are you *really* serious?"

The stranger seemed to be pondering the question before he gave a nod and a slight shrug.

Lester threw his hands up. "I'm not having this conversation." He turned and took a few steps down the driveway before turning around and practically shouting. "Who are you, man?"

The stranger had both hands out of his pockets now, holding them palms up and shaking his head. "So, when I asked for help, you didn't want to know me, but now that you think I'm responsible for a murder on your street, I all of a sudden matter."

"Are you kidding?" Lester placed one hand on his forehead. "I'm dreaming. I'm dreaming."

"Nah. This ain't a dream."

"Yes, it is."

"Not a dream, bro, sorry."

"Yes, it is. Shut up."

"I thought you wanted to know who I am. You're not making any sense right now, Lester."

Stomping, Lester came forward. "That's it." Less than a foot from the stranger's face, Lester pointed at him. "How do you know my name?"

"I know everyone's name on this street," the stranger said, unmoved.

"How?"

The stranger shrugged. "It's part of my job. You want to go get a cup of chai?"

Lester held his hands up in front of his face and screwed his face up again. "Cup of what? Man, are you serious? There is a dead guy in there, for goodness' sake."

The stranger turned slowly and looked into the house. When he turned back around, he looked confused. When he spoke, he did so slowly and angled his thumb behind him toward the house. "Lester, Wayne Burmeister is definitely dead. He killed himself because he was depressed and couldn't take it anymore, but why do you care? You didn't even know his name until I said it a second ago."

Lester started to walk slowly backwards. "Why am I talking to you?" He alternately touched his forehead and tossed his hands up helplessly. "What am I doing?"

The stranger held a hand out toward him. "Lester, wait."

"Dude, I don't know who you are, but I'm reporting you to the police when I get there. You better stay away from me and everyone in this neighborhood, man, because I'm telling you right now, it won't be pretty if you get caught around here again."

The stranger was shaking his head. "Lester, you really need to listen."

Lester was on the driver's side of his car, reaching for the door handle without looking away from the stranger.

"Are you kidding, man? I'm not listening to some psycho outside a dead man's house in the middle of the night. Whoever you are, you're sick. I'm not playing around. If I see you here again, you're dead on sight. You understand that? I'll shoot you myself, so you'd better hope the police find you first and take you in."

He looked away and got into the car, mumbling to himself. Lester stomped on the gas and sped away, not bothering to put on his seat-belt. The police station was ten minutes away. Leaving the stranger behind, Lester wondered if he would stop shaking in the time it took to get there.

Chapter 4

SEEING

RARELY IS SEEING BELIEVING, AND yet the world turns upon that misaligned axle, warping in orbit, spinning and gyrating from belief to belief, never understanding but clawing through tomes and relics for the slightest fragment of truth. The eyes lie to beliefs; beliefs lie to the eyes. Truth dances in the midst of a single moment, yet it is grasped at as if it wanders beyond the farthest stars, beyond the ethereal void where unanswered questions consolidate to dream up new tortures for the faithless.

Lester Sharp drove to the police station with the arthritic fingers of his weary mind stretched into that void, denying the lies his eyes told him, denying the reality his beliefs said could not be real. He scolded himself for leaving the strange man at the strange neighbor's home, likely hiding his murder and working to perfect the staged suicide. His mind told him the suicide was the truth; the face of the stranger told him there was more to it, more to all of this. Twice, he nearly turned around, almost went to confront the man about the heinous crime.

No wonder, then, that his eyes did not see what his mind told him were unmoving cars on the road, drivers frozen in place with hands on steering wheels, cell phones, radio buttons, or halfway through unkempt hair. No wonder his mind told him everything was normal when his eyes told him that he was driving in and out of the scarce traffic as if every other vehicle was standing still. But when he arrived at the police station, Lester's mental fingers retracted from beyond the invisible, infinite universe, and snapped back into place in time to tell him that he was the only animated feature of the still-life, midnight canvas of squad cars, police officers, people in handcuffs, and groups of voiceless conversations.

Lester pulled his car into a parking space, made sure that he was in it correctly while wondering why it mattered at all, and then got out slowly. He spent several minutes walking through the parking lot, going from person to person, group to group. Here, an officer with a Styrofoam cup of coffee up to his unmoving lips. There, an officer with his head angled toward his left shoulder, talking into the radio he held in his left hand that was also clipped to his shoulder. Some of them were frozen in laughter, some of them in mid-yawn. All of them were wax figures, statues in the imaginary world where Lester was now trapped.

Only, it wasn't imaginary. Neither was the dreadlocked stranger at the top of the stairs in front of the entrance to the police station. He was standing casually, leaning against a rail with his hands in his pockets.

"Yo! Figured it out yet, man?"

Lester stopped walking toward the steps and looked up at the stranger. He started to shout at the man but sighed and lowered his head instead. After another sigh, he looked up, moisture forming in his eyes, and shook his head.

The stranger nodded, pulled his hands from his pockets, and started walking down the steps slowly. He walked on air toward

Lester, though his black, white-striped Adidas sneakers were clearly making contact with the pavement. If he stopped, or if the pavement had been moving them and paused, Lester could not tell, but the stranger was now two feet away, looking into his eyes with his own icy blue orbs.

"Well?"

Lester swallowed. "Well, what?"

The stranger held his hands together in the shape of an imaginary pistol. "Where's your gun?" He smiled as he lowered his hands. "Didn't you say you were gonna shoot me on sight?" The stranger shrugged, grinning.

"Oh." Lester cleared his throat. Shaking his head, he breathed out a response. "I just want to know what's going on. I don't know who you are or what your deal is, but you've got me trapped in this nightmare."

"Is that what you think this is, Lester? A nightmare?"

"I don't care what it is." Lester was stepping back now, holding his hands up. "I just want this to be over, man. Let me out of whatever this is."

The stranger let out a breath and a laugh through his nostrils. Lester could handle no more. He charged for the man with his hands out in front of him, a growl leading the way. He grabbed whatever he could, felt what he thought might be a flannel shirt, fell into the stranger. He saw darkness, and then he saw the stranger's face peering down at him, silhouetted by the bright, yellowish orange street lamp far above them. As the stranger reached a hand down to him, Lester wondered how he had ended up on his back, how he had managed to let this man get away without noticing.

Lester took the extended hand and allowed the stranger to hoist him to his feet.

Calmly smoothing his clothes, the stranger spoke. "Lester, that was really rude."

Lester replied in a dazed, pausing tone. "What . . . is going . . . on?"

"Well, I thought you'd figure it out on your own, but I guess I wouldn't be here if you could do that." The stranger sighed loudly. "This is a moment, Lester. A single second of time in which all the world, except for you, is stopped. Paused. Frozen. Whatever you wanna call it, man." He shrugged and shook his head.

"That's not possible."

The stranger looked at Lester with contempt. "But here you are, like it or not, Lester, and my Boss says you get a chance to see the world like He does. You know, with, like, super vision glasses."

Lester screwed his face up. "Your Boss?"

The stranger nodded. "Yep. Think of yourself as, like, Ebeneezer Scrooge, and I'm that funny grasshopper."

Lester paused and furrowed his brow. "You mean the cricket, from *Mickey's Christmas Carol?*"

The stranger nodded. "Yeah, man. Jimmy."

"You mean, Jiminy?"

The stranger shrugged. "Whatever, man. Like I would know. Look, I'm your guide, alright?"

"No. Not alright. Not at all," Lester shouted. "And who is your Boss?"

The stranger tossed his hands up helplessly. "Really? How many people could freeze time?" He pinched his nose between his thumb and forefinger and groaned. "Why are you doing this to me? I gotta spell everything out for this dude."

"Who are you talking to?"

The stranger threw his arms up. "Who do you think, man?"

Lester patted the air in front of him. "Forget it. I can't even deal with that right now. What do you mean by me seeing a single moment of time?"

The stranger sighed, nodded slowly. Holding his arms out wide, he began to speak in a didactic tone.

"Look around you. All these people, doing their thing, living their lives. Day in, day out, and they don't even realize how connected they *really* are." He lowered his hands, easing one into his pants pocket.

"Do you have any idea what takes place in just a moment of time? Do you have a clue?"

Lester stood, speechless, staring at the stranger. The stranger shook his head. "Nah, course not. None of you do. None of you care either."

"You don't even know me!" Lester clenched his fists at his sides. "You don't know me. I don't know you. Now you're giving me a speech? Tell me what you want from me, so I can go home."

"Okay, see, you wanna get loud." The stranger turned and grabbed his face. He groaned before turning back around. "You wanna know?" The stranger stepped back.

Lester nodded after a brief pause, exhaling heavily.

"I want you to go inside, Lester." He turned sideways and motioned with his head toward the police station.

"What?"

"Go inside and see for yourself. Then we'll talk, man, 'cause I'm not fooling with you anymore."

Lester shook his head and let out a desperate laugh. "You're joking."

The stranger raised his free hand toward the station. "Dead serious. No games. Just go."

They stood. They stared. There was the slap of a hand against a leg, a sigh, and then Lester heard his feet on the pavement, walking past the stranger. Finding himself at the top of the steps to the station, he paused and turned to the stranger.

"I don't even know your name."

The stranger lifted his hands in the air and then let them fall to his sides. "If I tell you, will you go inside?"

A pause. A nod of the head. "Sure."

The stranger frowned and pointed at Lester. "You're pushing me, and that's a dangerous thing to do." He sighed. "Draven, man. My name is Draven."

Lester gave a weak nod and turned. "Draven?" he whispered to himself. The name was intimidating, and Lester wondered just how dangerous it really was to push this mysterious man.

The glass door into the police station opened without a sound, and Lester entered the brightly lit building cautiously. He paused, holding the door with his fingertips, and looked around. He was not sure what he was looking for, but he scanned from left to right and up and down as if something was going to jump out at him any second. It was late, so there were not many people inside the station, but he noticed the layout of the building right away.

The floor was covered in simple white, waxed tiles large enough for him to stand in, and they had been buffed and polished so perfectly that Lester could see the recessed ceiling lights without looking up. Directly to the front was a half-moon-shaped, dark mahogany desk covered in stacks of papers, candy wrappers, a stained coffee mug, and the arms of a police officer. His navy blue, pressed sleeves were resting in a pile of crumbs with one forearm draped in front of him and the other perpendicular to it and angled up in order to prop up his chubby, unshaven chin.

Lester stepped through the entrance, letting the door swing shut behind him as he walked past fake plants and small trees that had been cheaply arranged together in a futile attempt to create a pleasant atmosphere. Even with everything paused, Lester could imagine the myriad of smells mingling together in a depressing, noxious aroma. The bright lights seemed to him a humorless irony to the fact that the station held those that had been mostly caught committing criminal acts in the dark, but he hardly cared about that as he walked past the droopy-eyed officer on guard. Lester's attention had been drawn to the dramatic scene of the waiting area directly behind the desk, where a few men and women sat in an uncomfortable-looking square of black chairs with stiff backs, metal armrests, and cracked plastic seats.

An older-looking couple sat together at the far right, as far away from the rest of the people in the waiting area as possible. The man, rigidly erect in his chair, wore khaki-colored pants and shined shoes that matched his dark brown sweater and perfectly combed gray hair. The woman, most likely the man's wife as far as Lester could guess, was asleep on his shoulder uncomfortably. Her short, black hair was partly in her face, and her sweater and pants were nearly an identical match to his.

Lester was about to make his way around to them to get a closer look when the woman in front of him got his attention; at least, her appearance did. She was a small woman. Her dirty tennis shoes barely touched the floor, and her green, hooded sweatshirt was obviously borrowed from someone much larger than her. Her thin, blond hair was pulled back into a lazy pony tail that hadn't bothered to rope in the dry, spider web edges that seemed electrified by the way they were sticking out in every direction. Her face was blotchy red and fixed in the midst of a shout into the phone she was holding up to her face with fingers whose nails looked to have been chewed to just above the cuticles and dipped in mud. Lester walked over and kneeled in front of her, staring with his mouth open into her glazed-over eyes. Tears were frozen in streaks on her face, and Lester could see from the bags beneath her eyes that she was carrying exhaustion in them like luggage on a plane.

He forced himself to look away and stand up, to take in the view of the other visitors. A large man of Hispanic descent was slumped down in a chair with his face lit up by the blue glow of his smartphone. To the left of him, a skinny, pale-skinned man was slumped even further in his seat, staring at the ceiling; and a scantily dressed woman with wrinkled skin was pointing a long, pressed-on nailed finger in his face, which he appeared to be ignoring. The scene was surreal for Lester, watching people that may or may not be able to see him in the midst of their actions but frozen in the moment.

Shaking his head multiple times, Lester walked away from the waiting area and down a hallway to the left. He knew the layout of the police station from when Dillon had been arrested when they were in high school. Dillon had actually been innocent but arrested as an accomplice to a traffic incident that had resulted in the death of a young man. Dillon had been riding in the front passenger seat of a friend's car, on the way to a basketball game, when his friend had run over a man that had entered the crosswalk. In a state of shock and panic, they had fled from the scene; but a police car caught up to them ten minutes later, and both of them had been arrested.

Lester tried to remember the name of Dillon's friend as he walked down the hallway, but he was quickly distracted by the mannequin-like police officers on either side of the narrow hall. Several were frozen in mid-conversation; one was in mid-stride; and one was in the midst of drinking a sip of coffee.

He walked to the end of the hallway, unsure of what was guiding him in that direction, pausing randomly to look at people that seemed familiar, strange, there, and not there. A large, metal door with a small window at eye level was partly open at the end of the hallway, somewhat obstructed by a female police officer and a tall man in handcuffs. Lester paused to admire the contrast between the almost-tiny woman with short, faded hair in her sharp uniform and the long-haired, brown-toothed man that stood at least a foot and a half taller than her.

Again nudged by some force he could not explain, Lester moved past them both and slipped through the door. He was heading to the temporary holding cell, which he knew from visiting Dillon before his brother had been transported to the county jail. Inside the door, the room was large, and Lester found himself squinting to see clearly. He was in another narrow hallway lined by dingy white tables built into the walls beneath thick glass. Metal chairs were pushed underneath the tables, and wall phones were mounted to the left of each one. Lester walked past them without much notice, knowing that visiting hours ended long before midnight, and headed toward the other end of the large room to the holding cells.

They were simple, square rooms of thick concrete that could only be seen through windows that reminded him of something on a submarine mounted to the heavy doors. There were twelve cells, six to either side. Lester walked along the dark concrete floor, attempting some sort of creeping silence, as if he were sneaking up on someone. The entire scene felt cryptic, and he found himself rubbing an imaginary chill from his arms as he approached the first window. Inside, he saw two young men, barely more than eighteen, holding each other by the throats and collars. One of the men—a white man with on-purpose messy hair—had just punched the other—a black man with a shaved head—in the mouth. His fist was frozen just past the man's face, which was twisted dramatically to the side, and drops of blood hung frozen in mid-air.

Lester was partly mesmerized by the fact that such a moment was frozen before him like a true-life painting, but he had no trouble pulling himself away from the scene. He looked into the next cell and saw someone asleep on one of the small, spring cots. He couldn't make out any details because whomever it was had a thin blanket pulled over his body. The next cell held a man on a metal toilet, so Lester quickly moved on to the next, where a middle-aged man sat on a cot with his elbows on his thighs and his fingers folded together. His face was stoic, staring at the opposite wall in a blank, fixed contemplation.

Lester slowly moved away, feeling guilt for invading the privacy of the moment. The man was likely dealing with guilt or shame over his actions, or he was possibly facing anxiety that accompanied the fear of the unknown. Lester sighed and moved to the next cell reluctantly. Without emotion, he placed his fingers on the room of the tiny window of the next cell and peered in. What he saw made him gasp aloud. Inside the cell, blood was splattered all over one of the walls, trickling down the wall onto the concrete floor into the pool of blood that led to the open skull of a man. The body of the man was sprawled out awkwardly, arms and legs spread in either direction. Lying on his stomach, the dead man's face was turned toward Lester, and his open eyes pulled Lester into their cold, empty blackness.

"Poor guy just found out his wife is leaving him." Draven's voice was somber behind Lester, who turned to see the dreadlocked stranger. Draven stood with both hands in his pockets, shaking his head. "At least she came to see him, brought his son and everything, but she only did that to tell him he'd never see them again."

"What happened?" Lester asked in a shaky whisper.

Draven half-shook his head, half-nodded. "He couldn't find work. Sad story, man. No father; the dude's dad took off the night he was born. Mom worked all the time, still couldn't put enough food on the table, so he started robbing and slinging dope. He was making money, eating good for the first time; mom thought he was working, but then he got pinched for the armed robbery of a convenience store. By the time he got out of the joint, his mother was dead. He managed to get some work through one of those rehab programs, which is where he met his wife, but the hard-knock life was just too tempting. He's been in and out of prison for the last eight years for minor stuff; but that minor stuff adds up, and this time he's going away for a whole minute. Wife couldn't take it anymore, so she kept it real with him." He pointed toward the cell behind Lester. "That's how he reacted to the news."

"I don't want to see any more of this," Lester said. "What do I have to do for this to be over?"

"Do?" Draven said with a slightly higher pitched tone. "I told you, man, this is a glimpse. All there is for you to do is look; and for real, you ain't seen nothing yet, Lester."

Lester groaned.

Draven grabbed him gently by the shoulder. "Let's go; it's gonna be a long night." As they turned and walked out of the station, Draven asked Lester, "Hey, you want that chai?"

Chapter 5

A WALK IN THE PARK

The path most traveled is often the path least noticed. Practiced footsteps sink into the same sands of time with repeated depressions. Lamp posts, light poles, stop signs, and houses merge as one into mirror image collages that have been gazed upon, stared at, and ignored by a thousand nameless faces in a sea of travel and commerce. The details poured into concrete or the finite care carved into the blank doors of not-so-identical shops and homes is seldom seen by those that have been immersed into the temporal affairs of a world that spins and spins, unconcerned for its sickly passengers. Spinning in the midst of such a still mirage was Lester, dizzy from the lack of motion in the town he grew up in and never saw.

He stood outside a glass-front coffee shop in an old part of the town with his arms folded. It had been awkward at first, standing next to the frozen figure of a police officer, but Lester had eventually simply shrugged his shoulders and given up trying to make any sense out of this night. This area of town, with its old store fronts and independently owned small businesses, had once been his favorite place to go. He and Dillon often went there to get a coffee and walk along the sidewalk outside the shops observing things, watching people.

A string of small bells made a jingling sound behind him, and he turned to watch as Draven came out of the coffee shop with two paper cups in his hands. Lester thought it was strange to see the dread-locked man with baggy jeans and flannel shirt coming out of a shop that normally catered to people in business attire or the elderly with their hundred-dollar sweaters and orthopedic shoes. The man he still considered a stranger walked up to him with a smile and reached out one of the cups to him. He took it with a nod of his head and sighed.

"You're a barista, too?" Lester asked before taking a sip. The hot, sweet taste of spiced chai tea instantly soothed his tense nerves, and he let out another sigh.

"Isn't everybody with a master's degree?"

Lester nearly spit his second sip, pulling the cup away quickly in reaction to Draven's statement. He looked at the stranger with his mouth and eyes opened wide. Draven was chuckling and trying to take a sip from his own cup at the same time.

"Nah, I'm playing with you, dude." He paused from speaking long enough to take a drink. "We don't exactly fit in around those college campuses." He pointed with the same hand that was holding the cup toward the park across the street. Both men began to walk slowly in that direction, alternately sipping from their cups and talking.

"We?"

Draven looked at Lester out of the corner of his eye. "Still haven't figured it out yet?"

Lester walked in silence for a few steps, reluctant to answer. "I think I have," he finally said, "but I don't think I can admit it to myself."

Draven laughed. "It's cool, man. You've seen a lot in one night." He took a drink and then started talking before he'd finished swallowing. "This is a really nice park, Lester. Why don't you come here anymore?"

Lester stopped and turned to fully face Draven. "Anymore? How much do you know about me?"

Draven shrugged. "About as much as I know about everybody else in this town."

"And how is that?"

Draven motioned toward a park bench to his left and walked over to it. Lester reluctantly followed. "Because it's the same in every town," he said once he'd sat down. "Take you, for example." He set his cup on the ground and propped both of his arms on the back of the bench so that he could lean back. "You didn't even notice all the people we passed because you're so busy trying to figure out your own situation."

Lester opened his mouth to respond, but then he began to look around. To his amazement, there were people all over the park and the street in front of it where they had just passed. Cars were parked on the street with people in them or about to get into them. A man was leaning against a light pole, talking on his cell phone. Another man and a woman were walking together, holding hands. A homeless man was stretched out on another park bench with a newspaper draped over his chest and part of his bearded face. Sitting on a swing, alone, was a boy that could not have been more than fourteen. His hands were folded in front of him, and he was looking at the ground. All of them were frozen in place like mannequins.

"His mom kicked him out, man." Lester looked back to Draven and saw him shaking his head and looking toward the boy. "His dad left a year ago, and he's been in and out of trouble since. Classic case, you know?" He looked up at Lester with watery eyes.

Lester shrugged. "Everybody's got problems."

Draven snorted. "True." He sat forward and folded his hands in his lap. "Tell me, Lester, did you ever notice these people when you and Dillon used to come here?"

Lester started to raise his hands, started to shrug, then gave up. "I, I guess. I don't know."

Draven nodded. "That's what I thought. You do know it's midnight, right? What do you think's gonna happen to a fourteen-year-old boy in a park this late at night?"

Lester scoffed. "Come on. In this town? It's practically a sitcom from the fifties."

"No, Lester, not at all." He waited for Lester to sit on the bench next to him. "Admit it. You didn't even know there were homeless people in this town up until a second ago."

Lester was silent, but he nodded when Draven kept staring at him.

Draven pointed past Lester's face. "See that?" Lester followed the direction of his finger toward the far side of the park. A group of teenagers were emerging from a small copse of trees. They were male and female, dressed for warmer weather and carrying beers and bottles. "The kid on the swing got into it with one of them over a girl in school today. The fight is the reason his mom kicked him out, and now he's about to have to deal with all of them."

Lester stammered through a shocked reply. "Okay, but, but he'll be alright, won't he?" He looked back and forth between Draven, the boy, and the teenagers. "I mean, it's just a fight. Kids fight. He'll be a little busted up, but then it'll all be over. He'll probably end up friends with them when it's all over."

Draven shook his head. "You're a special kind of stupid, Lester. That may be how things were settled when you were a kid, but not these days."

"What do you mean?"

Draven reached down, picked up his cup, sat back, and let out a groan. "Man, it's all about pushing it to the edge now. It's like people can't take being slightly offended, you know? You mess with me . . . bang!" He motioned as if he was squeezing the trigger of an imaginary gun. "It's like life don't matter no more."

Lester sprang to his feet. "Wait, what?" Tea sloshed out of his cup with his arm movements. "Are you saying they're about to kill that kid for messing with a girl?" He turned in a frantic half-circle to the boy, then back to Draven. "No. Come on, man, that's crazy." Draven nodded but did not reply. "And you're just going to sit there, drinking your tea?"

Draven never took his eyes off Lester as he slowly lifted the cup to his lips, took a drink, and lowered it casually. "Ain't that what you do?" He shrugged and rested the cup in the lap of his legs, which he had crossed.

"What?" Lester was shaking his head. "No, it's not. I don't sit by and let this kind of stuff happen."

Draven nodded. "Sure, you do. You see it on the news when you're flipping through channels looking for the football game. You scroll past it on your social media. You roll your eyes at it every time you see one of these kids with their pants sagged below their butt. Man, you've been sitting back your whole life, drinking your tea, while kids like that go into the gutter. Don't look at me like *I'm* the problem."

Lester took a deep breath, so deep that it felt like his chest was going to pop. He looked around, unsure of how to respond. His gaze fell over the boy; but when he saw the grim expression frozen on the boy's face, he had to look away. He saw the small mob of teenagers, none of them old enough to drive, and he suddenly felt sick. He slowly turned his body and head at the same time until he was looking at the homeless man asleep on the bench again. Lester thought the man looked dead. His left arm was hanging down so that his hand was draped on the ground lifelessly, and the pause in time prevented the man's chest from rising and falling.

"How long has he been like that?" Lester asked, pointing to the man.

Draven had stood up and was walking up to stand beside Lester. "A long time. Don't you remember giving him some change about six years ago?"

Lester immediately shook his head in reply. "No. I feel like I don't remember any of this, like I'm seeing this park for the first time." He turned his head slightly to the left and looked into Draven's startlingly blue eyes. How odd, he thought.

Draven nodded. "Maybe so, Lester, maybe so."

Chapter 6

THE CRACKS

THERE IS A FIRST TIME for everything to be seen that is seen, but rarely is anything truly noticed when it is being seen for the first time. As Lester walked with Draven through the city, he knew that he was noticing everything for the first time, even though he had seen most of them many times already. The cracks in the sidewalk became gaping canyons before him. The multi-colored sea of cars, trucks, and motorcycles seemed to dull with every step he took, becoming trapped under layers of rust and poverty the farther away from his home they traveled. The slow decay he knew was inevitable rapidly descended upon every building until the buildings became older buildings and, then, abandoned buildings, surrounded by condemned houses with nailed-up warning signs that told passersby to stay on the other side of the decay where the occupants of such places are never seen.

He was surrounded by the decay, by the forgotten streets that inbred violence and carelessness. He noticed it on the multi-colored faces of individuals, groups, and miniature mobs that should have been asleep in the condemned buildings that had neglected to nail up their signs. He noticed it when the sea of cars slowly turned into a thinning wave washed up on a sandless beach that had not seen the tide rise before. He noticed it in the silence, the soundless echo that even Draven seemed to respect, to reverence, and to loathe all at once.

He noticed it in the weight of the air and the almost-absent beating of his heart.

"How is it that I've never seen all of this before?" Lester asked Draven without looking at him, continuing his soft, concrete, scraping stride.

Draven sniffled. "You've seen it. You've just never really paid attention to it before. A glance down a side street at a stop sign, a quick stare at the houses below the ramp to the highway. It's been here, waiting to be noticed."

Lester nodded but did not reply to the answer that he had already surmised. "So, where are we going?"

Draven stopped and pointed straight ahead. "There."

A couple hundred feet away, a crowd had gathered at one of the larger intersections between Martin Luther King Jr. Boulevard and Washington. Lester immediately took note of a contrast between the crowd that was unevenly divided. On the left, a large group of men, women, and young teenagers of both sexes stood in either unnecessarily loose or tight clothing of different brands and colors. On the right, a smaller group of twelve men and four women all wore dark blue jeans and red t-shirts. Walking closer to the human statue display, Lester saw that the shirts on the right were all the same design. He approached the man closest to him—an older, familiar-looking man with a neatly trimmed beard and large glasses. The shirt had large, bold letters in white that read THE WATCHMEN on the front.

As he walked between the two frozen crowds, he quickly noticed that the faces on the left were angry or held expressions of mocking. The faces on the right were a mixture of smiles, fear, and stoicism. At the end of the group, one of the men—a tall man of African descent—was standing with his eyes closed, and his shoulders looked slightly raised, as if he had just tensed himself up before time had stopped. In front of him was a slightly shorter man, also of African descent, wearing a tank top and torn jeans. He had a fist pulled back as if he was about to punch the man in the red shirt, and his face was screwed up into a frozen snarl. Lester felt Draven brush past his shoulder, watched him walk in between the two. Draven turned around and looked at Lester for a long, uncomfortable moment, then turned to the man to Lester's left. He reached out and grabbed the man by both shoulders, let out a frustrated sigh, and then twisted the man's body an inch toward Lester. He then turned toward the man in the red shirt and tilted his head a half-inch away from Lester. When he had finished, he smiled and walked away, past Lester, and kept walking.

Lester turned quickly and shouted after him, "Where are you going?"

Draven kept walking, but replied without looking back, "There's more to see, Lester." He motioned with his hand for Lester to follow, never turning around or looking back.

Lester ran to catch up with him. "What was that?"

"What did it look like?"

"I don't know."

Draven chuckled. "Man, shocker." He stopped and turned to face Lester, and then pointed toward the crowd they had just left. "The people in the red shirts, they come out here every Friday night around this time. They invite people to their church, talk to them about God, try to help them, that sort of thing."

Lester hesitated. "They look familiar."

Draven shook his head and rolled his eyes. "They should, man. That's your people, your church."

Lester screwed up his face and took a half-step back. "My church?"

"Yeah, man, the one you haven't been to since you got your little business off the ground? That church."

Lester looked down slightly and sighed. "I think I already knew that."

Draven replied in an irritated tone. "I think you already knew a lot of things, Lester." He tossed his hands up and then started walking again. Lester stayed where he was, but he looked back to the two men that Draven had moved.

When he had taken in the scene once more, he turned his head to Draven and shouted a question. "Why did you move those two?"

Without looking back, Draven shouted his response. "Because the dude was praying, man."

Lester looked back at the two men. He next question was to himself, almost under his breath. "For protection?"

Draven shouted a reply to the question he could not possibly have heard. "For the one about to hit him."

Lester lowered his head, and his shoulders sagged. At his feet, he noticed a crack in the sidewalk.

Chapter 7

TAPESTRIES

OFTEN, THOSE THAT TRAVEL MOST are the most unaware people in the world. The wandering soul seeking the myths and fables of the mountains and seas to inspire songs and poetry too often misses the stories hidden within the caves. The seafaring man is open to the vast expanses of the deep waters but becomes less-grounded to the small, significant details of a single grain of sand washed up by those waters. Likewise, the bleary-eyed consumers of modern life see the buildings and houses as a blur that streaks past them, while caffeine-drifting their way from job to home and home to job without ever seeing the tapestries of hopeless frustration and lawlessness painted in the alleys between those buildings and houses.

Lester's chai-induced trance had been fleeting, and his finally-focused eyes were now fixed upon tapestries of poverty and shame as he walked with the enigmatic stranger from alley to alley. For the first time in his life, Lester saw the filth of streets not cared for by the city because commerce was not prevalent in the part of town he now traversed. He saw the decay of it all, felt the depression in the stale air that had been frozen by the stagnation of generational poverty long before this night's time lock had existed. He saw beyond drug dealers and saw the results. He felt the burden of the fatherless wandering the streets, alone with terror and defeat etched in their eyes, and Lester thought it strangely appropriate that time had frozen them because, to his reckoning, they were locked in a timeless cycle of miserable life that would eventually give birth to uneventful death.

Nothing, however, could have prepared him for the gruesome scene painted on the ultimate tapestry of man's depravity that he and Draven found down one particular side street. As they rounded the corner, dark pools lay blotched on the concrete, shining an ominous red in the slivers of pale moonlight. He instinctively knew the pools were blood, not water, and Lester wondered if he was, in fact, the mannequin in that moment because he could not bring himself to move.

"It's a glimpse, Lester," Draven calmly said at his side. "You don't get out of this if you don't see what my Boss says you need to see."

Voice trembling, Lester replied. "I'm not looking up." He clenched his eyes shut. "I don't care. I'm not looking."

He heard Draven sigh harshly. "I know you don't want to look. I don't either, but you have to."

Eyes still clenched tightly, Lester shook his head back and forth rapidly, squeezing his hands into fists and then releasing them nearly as rapidly as his head shook. "I can't. I can't."

A hand firmly but gently gripped his shoulder. "Open your eyes."

Lester became still, forced himself to calm through the aid of the hand on his shoulder and the uncharacteristically soothing voice at his side. After another moment to allow his breathing to steady, he slowly opened his eyes and lifted his head from the spilled blood. Lying just a few feet away, a woman was awkwardly spread out on the ground. Dark hair covered her face and neck, but not as dark as the numerous stains on her dingy, pink shirt. Across her stomach were the multiple smears of blood that had been violently shed by stab wounds. Darker still was the blood from her naked privates that began a trail to the pools at Lester's feet, a trail interrupted by the tiny mass of unbreathing flesh and blood that lay unmoving forever on the cold concrete.

Lester ran, in no particular direction, until he collided with bricks he did not see. He fell away enough to get his arms up and to brace his body as it began to lurch beyond his control. Hot, acidic bile rose from the pit of his stomach and erupted from his mouth and throat, then splattered on the black street. He lurched and wretched, his body becoming wracked in agony as his insides were spilled on the ground that had become the grave of the woman and her child. It felt like an eternity of vomiting; and when his body could offer no more, he turned to run from the alley, but he ran into something else. Not a wall this time, but just as firm and immovable. He tried not to look into Draven's eyes, tried not to notice their bright reflection of the moon despite the nearly impenetrable dark of the night; but the pull to the stranger's face was too much, too necessary.

"There's more."

"Get me out of here." Lester suddenly did not care that tears were burning his eyes. He no longer cared if this man heard the wailing in his voice or noticed that he was pleading. "I can't do this, Draven. I never asked for this."

Strong hands gripped both sides of his face and forced him to look into Draven's. "They didn't ask for this either." He paused. "Now go."

Lester growled and jerked to his right, snatching himself from the inhuman grip. Practically in slow motion, he turned back to the woman—head first, then torso, and finally feet. He inched his way forward at first, then gradually took his first full step until a glint of metal caught his peripheral vision. Lying a few feet from the woman was a stiletto blade, covered in blood that had a single drop frozen in mid-drip between the steel and the concrete. Lester walked over to it, and then began to look around at the rest of the alley. There was more light at the end, and far more to see, he quickly realized.

Lester was running before he fully saw what he had thought had only been imagined. He was kneeling at the side of a man sprawled on the ground and lying in a similar pool of blood to the woman's before he knew that he had stopped running. He had seen the people that had gathered around the dead man in the T-intersection of the street that he had previously been unaware of. He was up and backing away, shaking his head in slow motion as he looked back and forth between the faces in the small crowd.

A voice, small and calm, stopped him. "Whole worlds exist between these streets." Draven spoke evenly, nearly emotionless. "Stories no one has bothered to read except the people that don't care enough to tell them. These alleys are like books on a shelf in a locked bookstore, man. Nobody's reading these."

Lester turned around and took a long look at the man, standing comfortably with his hands in his pockets. "Doesn't this bother you?" He asked with a slight shake of his head and a helpless raising of his hands.

"Oh, it bothers me." Draven's facial expression did not budge. "But does it really bother you?"

Lester pointed to the alley behind Draven. "Did you not see the way I reacted just now?"

Draven shrugged. "I've seen it a million times, man. People see something like that; natural reaction is to do what you did. Congratulations, dude, you're human. You got grossed out, and your gag reflex kicked in. So what? You think that equals compassion?" Draven laughed, cynically. "Give me a break. The only thing you're thinking about right now is how much more of this you have to see."

"You don't know that."

Draven shrugged. "Like I said, seen it a million times."

Lester clenched his teeth and shook his head. "I don't care what you think of me. This is horrible, and it bothers me. I don't have to justify my reactions to you."

"You're right about that." Draven nodded and pushed his bottom lip out. "You're surely right about that."

"Whatever," Lester said, snapping back. "Are we done?"

Draven smiled. "Nah. We're just getting started."

Lester groaned. He hesitated for as long as he could before following Draven. Strangely, leaving the alley he could not wait to be away from suddenly seemed worse. He wondered what could possibly be worse than that tragic, still-life painting of death. Revulsion drove him onto the main street again. He found Draven leaning against the wall of one of the buildings, one foot propped against the wall and his arms folded. He was looking straight ahead, nonchalantly staring at nothing, yet gazing deeply into the air before him.

"Where now?" Lester spoke flatly.

Draven turned his head slightly. "You tired of walking?"

Lester screwed his face up. "Well, yeah." Unsure of what to say but uncomfortable with the silence that followed because Draven did not respond, Lester offered, "Do you want to go back to the police station and get my car?"

Draven gave a wide, closed-mouth smile. "Actually, I was thinking of something a little bit faster."

Before Lester could respond or react, Draven stood straight up, unfolded his arms, and stepped forward. He moved impossibly fast, reaching his arm around to place his hand in the small of Lester's back, and then Lester felt himself being pushed toward the building. He yelled in protest as Draven's incredibly strong hand compelled him into the wall. He could not resist the power of the man, the sheer strength unlike anything that he had ever encountered. Positively mortified, Lester stared wide-eyed at the rapidly approaching bricks he was about to smash into; but then they were no longer in front of him, and he could no longer feel anything.

He was suddenly passing through the bricks, and his body felt completely weightless. The hand continued to push him. For reasons he could not explain, he did not try to resist, somehow knowing that he could not. His body was void of sensation, and his eyes detected impenetrable darkness. He knew that he was moving, but he could not feel movement. He knew there was a strong hand pushing him, but he could no longer feel it. And then, as quickly as he had been thrust into the wall and darkness, he emerged on the other side, into light. He saw a blur of broken furniture and items strewn across a torn carpet, but it all became a streak of dull colors as he approached the far wall of the tiny room.

Darkness again. Light once more. Still, the hand pushed and, still, he was weightless as he passed through house after house and building after building, over streets and intersections without his feet touching the asphalt. He sped faster and faster until there were fewer buildings, scattered houses, and then no houses, and he was moving like a rocket, diagonally over fields, through trees, over a tiny stream. Before him, the larger city to his not-so-small town loomed like a threatening gray tower of steel and glass; and then he was in that city, and through it, down several flights of underground stairs, over a concrete slab filled with scattered pedestrians and newspaper kiosks, through the thin wall of a poorly lit subway car; and then he stopped.

He stood perfectly still, filled with gravity once more, and all was still. He heard the shuffling of feet, saw Draven come from his side and then sit in a torn, green-cushioned bench. After folding his hands in his lap, he nodded his head upward slightly. Lester moved robotically backwards, unsure step after unsure step until the back of his legs bumped into something stiff and poorly cushioned. He sat down without looking back, keeping his eyes focused on the calm, dreadlocked stranger sitting across the aisle from him.

"Hang on tight, Lester," Draven said with a smug smile. "We have a lot to see tonight."

The subway train began to move, slowly at first, and Lester felt his eyes opening wider and wider as Draven's smile stretched even farther, and then the train was moving faster, faster than any subway train should move. Draven threw his head back and laughed; Lester covered his face with his hands and buried both in his lap. He could not look up or out the windows, terrified to know where they were going, and more than terrified as he wondered who, or what, was driving the train.

Chapter 8

THE WORLD NEXT DOOR

FOR CENTURIES, MAN HAS LOOKED into the heavens with wonder and awe, seeking to understand the vast expanse of innumerable solar systems and a universe that stretches seemingly forever, and yet man has rarely turned the telescope to gaze in awe below the surface of his own world. Humanity gleefully hopes to explore, inhabit, and conquer worlds beyond reach, while its own world drifts through the emptiness of the galaxy, losing its explorers and inhabitants by the thousands daily. Mankind's eyes look up longingly to the moon and planets, separated by the great deep, the blackness of space, while navigable oceans of nearly infinite wonders are all that separates man from cultures and worlds they have never seen except through pictures, making them just as allusive and worth exploring as the cosmos.

Such worlds were beginning to open up to Lester, though the common fears that accompanied exploration had temporarily crippled him. He sat up after a long while and looked in every direction. Draven was still sitting across the aisle in front of him, but he had rested his head against the window and fallen asleep. Lester looked beyond the strange man to the window behind him. Beyond the thin glass, translucently lit by the emergency lights of the subway car, was a dark blanket of water—deep, thick water—which he was instantly convinced flowed beyond the train to eternity. He got up with a start and ran over to the window. The train, still moving incredibly fast despite being in deep waters, was steady enough for him to walk and not fall, but the feeling of dizziness immediately assaulting his senses told him that he needed to walk carefully.

He gingerly approached the windows, pressed his fingertips against it, and looked into the red and green-highlighted depths. Enchantment was instantaneous and complete for Lester as he looked into the eye of a massive blue whale that was frozen in the midst of the waters just barely above the view of the train. As he looked up and down, he found other species of fish all frozen in motion. The colors were like nothing he had seen before, shimmering and brilliant. Somehow, the scene was calming. Though he realized that he was actually in a subway train that was streaming at the speed of a bullet through an ocean on no tracks, Lester seemed not to be able to notice anything beyond the colors and life outside the windows. Finding himself continuously amazed by the things he had seen in a never-ending night but also becoming aware that he was less able to be shocked, Lester slid his hands from the window and took a step back.

"It's a world full of wonders, isn't it?" Draven's voice to his left pulled Lester from his trance. He turned to look at his unlikely traveling partner, still sitting with his head resting against the window and his eyes closed.

"At least some things are still worth looking at," Lester replied after a few moments. He stepped back and slid his hands in his pockets. He had somehow gotten used to the speed with which the train was moving through the water.

"Why aren't the other things worth looking at?" Draven kept his eyes closed but shrugged slightly. "What, something's uncomfortable, so you just turn away?"

"Do you ever not lecture?"

Draven gave a slight laugh in response at first, then opened his eyes and sat forward. "It's not a lecture, man, just a question."

Lester groaned. "Who wants to look at people suffering and dying?"

Draven nodded. "Yeah, who wants to see that? But did you ever stop and think that maybe the people suffering and dying don't wanna see that either?"

Lester turned his head quickly and stared at Draven, but he had no response; so he slowly turned his attention back to the waters, which had brightened and seemed less deep somehow. He felt the train shifting upward to his right, and he had to move back to his seat to prevent himself from sliding down the aisle. Once he was sitting down and holding onto the armrest of the bench seat, he looked at Draven and spoke.

"It's not like I don't care. Of course, I care."

"Man, define care."

"I don't have to define anything, especially to you; I don't even know you."

"Okay. Fair enough. But check this out: when's the last time you thought about something other than your shop or how much work *you're* putting into it?"

Lester shook his head. "It's my job. I have to think about it, and I have to put time into it." Draven was nodding with a skeptical expression. "Do you know that I have employees? What if I let the business fall apart? What happens to them? I keep us in business, which means

I make sure they have a paycheck, which means I'm putting food on their tables. Don't tell me I don't care."

Draven was silent for a moment, then leaned back. "So, how's that hospital bill for Davis coming?"

"What?" Lester scrunched up his face and cocked his head back.

Draven pointed at Lester, then dropped his hand back into his lap. "You know, Art Davis. His kid's dealing with radiation treatment for cancer."

"Art Davis doesn't even work for me anymore. He hasn't worked for me in over a month."

"Oh, that's right." Draven slowly nodded. "You fired him for missing work. My mistake."

Lester felt a lump in his throat and a sudden uneasiness in his stomach—not one caused by the motion of the train. He mentally made the connection to why Art had been late so much and groaned. He leaned forward and put his elbows on his thighs so that he could put his face in the palms of his hands. He groaned. He swallowed the lump back. He rubbed his face, putting pressure on his eyes before looking up at Draven with his hands still supporting his chin.

"I didn't know."

"I know that, Lester. I also know that you didn't know your manager and his wife are sleeping in separate rooms because she won't speak to him. That tends to happen when a husband's never home or spends all his time on the phone when he is home. I also know that you didn't know that your manager wasn't responding to you tonight because Bill had to go pick up Rashaad, one of your mechanics, from the interstate because he and his daughter—the one he's raising by himself—ran out of gas. That happens when you don't have gas money, by the way."

Draven paused, leaned forward, and then finished. "But at least you're putting food on his table."

Lester wanted to strangle this man, to rip his throat out and stomp on it; but he knew he would never even get close. He knew he was not the one in control of his situation, that he was at the mercy of the man and the powerful, unknown Forces controlling him that night.

"I'll look into it." He looked away.

"No, you won't, Lester, and I'm not here for you to tell me what you're gonna do and what you're not gonna do. I'm just your guide."

"Then why all the speeches?" Lester tried but failed to keep the edge out of his tone.

"I see it, and you don't. My job is to show you."

"Yeah, well, I'm pretty busy these days. Have you seen that with your little spy cameras or whatever you've got keeping tabs on my personal life and the lives of everyone else? I see things. I care. I know what's going on in the world. Just because I don't know all the details doesn't mean I don't know."

"It must be exhausting lying to yourself this much." Draven held his hand up to stop Lester from protesting verbally. "Nah, man, just listen. You're like these sea creatures, like a little fish. You swim around in the water—deep in it, too—but you never come up for air. But you're human, and you have to breathe, so you're also like that whale back there. You come up to collect some air, but you don't really have time to look around. You see that the ocean is still there, but you can't name the waves or tell whether it's night or day."

"I'm pretty sure a whale can tell when it's daylight," Lester said sarcastically.

"Don't change the subject. Apart from your shop and your desk at home, there's only one other place in the world you know even exists, and that's because the one person, other than yourself, that you *do* think about is there."

Lester was quiet, then furrowed his eyebrows. "Dillon?"

Draven's nod was barely noticeable. "Yeah. Dillon. You think about your brother, and you worry because he's in a war zone; but that's all you think about beyond your tight, little circle."

"But doesn't that prove I care about something besides myself?"

"Trust me." Draven stood up. "When this is all over, we'll find out."

Lester stared up at him, lost for words.

Draven signaled for him to stand up. "Come on. We're almost there."

Lester reluctantly stood up as he looked out the windows. The train was no longer in water, though he had not noticed the transition to the surface. "Where are we going?" He saw fields that spread out past the train farther than any he had ever seen before. Short trees and shrubs made up the only, sparse vegetation of the sand-colored land outside. Small homes, huts made of gray wood and scraps, began to appear interspersed as the train slowed.

"We're on the Horn of Africa," Draven said as the train came to a gentle stop. "You're about to see where we're going." The doors of the train opened. Draven nodded toward them, and Lester dejectedly walked through them.

Chapter 9

FEELING

THE ADAGE OF EXPERIENCE BEING the best teacher is one that can be spoken only by those that have been thrust into the subject of the saying by time and circumstance. Experiencing pain cannot be explained or illustrated and still carry the same meaning as the breaking of bones, the piercing or tearing of skin, or the searing agony of extreme heat or cold upon exposed flesh. And yet, empathy does not always require one to walk through the same fire as another, for the pain of one experience can sometimes translate into others and take one to a place of equal sorrow, hurt, betrayal, or despair. The factory worker struggling to make ends meet and who has not eaten well in some time can see the destitute state of the homeless woman and imagine the great length of discomfort, fear, hunger, and hopelessness the displaced endures.

Lester felt the sorrow in the frozen air before he stepped through the thin doors of the displaced subway train, knew the despair that hung limply from the hearts of the people he had not even seen before his shoes ground into the hot sand. Crunching the dusty grain beneath him as he walked seemed to add to, rather than break, the enchantment that had instantly placed him under a spell of mourning the moment Draven had told him to go outside. Under that spell, the heat upon his skin from the naked sun seemed like nothing more than the soft amount of radiation generated by a tiny light bulb. Walking gingerly with half-strided, unmeasured steps, he found himself looking into the close-eyed, dark-skinned faces of nearly starved men, women, and children—less than twenty of them down on their knees, hands and arms up and out in front of their faces. He spun left and right and saw the sadistic, sparkling eyes of other dark-skinned men all wearing red and white hijabs around their heads and covering their faces. The black and brown rifles were above their heads, several of them with frozen balls of fire frozen at the end of the muzzles and bullets in mid-flight.

The two lines—one standing, one kneeling—had formed a crescent in front of a small, mud block building in a dirt field of sparse vegetation, whose pattern was only broken up by a few scattered huts of the same roofless, doorless ilk. A lone tree without leaves stood like a tiny tower beside the hut, and the woman hanging by the neck from it was so frail that she seemed to be somewhere between a sickly scarecrow and a diseased extension of the dead branches of the rotting tree. At her feet lay the decapitated body of a man whose head was now only connected to his mutilated neck by an unmoving stream of dark blood. Lester hardly needed to scan to the right of the man to see the cross carved into the side of the frame that would have held a door if the kneeling vagrants surrounding him could have afforded one. Neither did he need to ask Draven why it was dark and wet, for the perpetrators of the darkening of the cross were still present, their cans of gasoline held in mid-douse by the second hand of time, held by Lester's tortured glimpse and watery gaze.

Lester winced as his knees struck the hot sand, and he caught himself from falling to his face with his outstretched palms. He was gasping for air and fighting back giant sobs. It felt as if the air had left him, had simply moved away and left him in a vacuum void of oxygen, and he wondered if he would ever breathe again. He tried in vain to force his eyes up, tried to look into the terrified faces of the real-life mannequins that were an eye blink away from death, but grief and cowardice were far too heavy for him to lift.

He crawled on hands and knees to a young boy, one of the few that had been either too brave or too naive to close his eyes. Lester looked into those dark brown irises, and there was suddenly no fighting the sobs, the rivers of water dammed behind his own. Hand stretched out to the boy he had never met, salty tears blurring his vision, Lester recognized the face. It was the same face he had seen on countless commercials asking for help. It was the same face on the cover of the unread magazine buried beneath a stack of unopened bills and the latest letter from Dillon, the magazine he received every quarter and never bothered to read. It came from The Voice of the Martyrs, an organization that sends aid and workers to the persecuted Church around the world. Lester remembered registering to get the magazines.

"Never read any of them, do you?"

Lester closed his eyes and lowered his hand to the ground. After taking a breath to steady his chest from heaving, he responded. "Another lecture?"

Draven's voice was even, his reply expected. "Not a lecture; just a question."

Lester clenched his jaw tightly and pushed himself to his feet. Not bothering to dust off his hands and knees, he turned and walked toward Draven, who was standing between two of the armed men with his hands in his pockets. The contrast between him and the other men was striking, but Lester barely noticed. He waited until he was a foot away from his guide before stopping and pointing into his face.

"You've got all these questions for me. Well, I've got some for you, *man*." Draven's face was stoic, unchanged. "How is it that you see all of this and do nothing? What can I do about this or anything else you've shown me? I'm one man. Maybe if I had what you have, I could do something about all of this, and maybe I'm better than you because I actually would!"

Draven took in a long drink of air, then let it out slowly. "Put your hand down, Lester." Lester lowered his hand obediently. "All that I have?"

Lester gestured toward the train. "Yeah, all that you have. Like the super-powered magic school bus over there or the ability to walk through walls and fly. You can go around the world any time you want."

Draven laughed and walked around Lester, who had to turn to follow him. "That's what you think?" Draven walked slowly, looking at each of the people individually as he spoke. "Nah, man. I can't do anything anytime I want, and I sure don't get to go riding around in borrowed subway trains through the ocean. I mean, if I could, I'd never do my job."

"Then, what do you do?" Lester asked.

Draven stopped walking and turned. "I told you, Lester. It's a glimpse. You think I snatch people out of their lives every second of every day and go around the world?" He shook his head. "First time for me, too, man. But back to you. How come you never read those magazines?"

Lester looked down at his feet and shook his head slowly. "It's just too hard."

Draven was nodding when Lester looked back up. "Yeah, but I bet it'd be hard for them to read magazines about what you and the rest of the Church in the first world are going through."

Lester was silent for nearly a minute, surveying the scene. "What can I do? Can't you do something, like the way you did before?"

Draven shook his head. "Like I told you before, Lester, the man I helped had someone praying for him." He pulled his hands from his pockets and walked toward Lester, patting him on the shoulder in passing.

Without looking over his shoulder, Lester asked: "Would it change anything?"

Draven's voice sounded distant in his response. "Sometimes, it does. I don't get to know." By the sound of a sliding door opening behind him, Lester knew that Draven had boarded the subway train again.

Lester walked around the half-moon-shaped gathering again, looking into the faces of the victims with guilt and compassion. Each time he saw one of the aggressors, he stared at them with contempt; but then he felt the same guilt, and he knew that none of them were really that much different. He walked over to the tree, stared into the contorted face of the woman who had been hanged. It was bloated, and her unmoving arms and legs were limp. He held back bile in his throat as he looked down at the beheaded man and walked past him toward the building. He wanted to reach out and remove the gas cans from the men splashing it all over the tiny hut, but he knew that he would not be able to touch them. He walked into the dark, little hut, found it to be a single room that had been trashed, and walked around. There was not much to destroy, which was the only strange positive note that Lester could find as he looked at some scattered books and papers along with an overturned drum set and a small podium.

Kneeling down, he saw that the podium had been holding a Bible. It was open but torn. Lester was surprised to find it written in English, but he was too overwhelmed to read what was on the page. He stood up and took in one last view of the dirt floor, the palm and straw roof, and the dark, cool mud walls; and then he walked out into the sunlight again. His steps back to the subway train were heavy, and he plopped down into his seat once he was back on board without looking at Draven. He heard the door shut as he leaned his head back against the window and closed his eyes.

Chapter 10

AROUND THE WORLD

SILENCE IS FAR TOO OFTEN an elusive, nearly mythical force that becomes hidden in the midst of the many conflicting brush strokes on the canvas of life. The flat brush bullies silence into the background only to be fanned too thin to grasp before the round brush twists it and manipulates it into the indiscernible elements of meetings, nonstop entertainment, empty calls and emptier conversations over microwaved dinners and midnight surfs across the chaotic and unpredictable waves of cyberspace. Silence is the hope of the overworked and the temporary solace of the resting, but ultimately, it is the enemy of those evading truth. Silence exposes the core, the innermost depths of wanderers that have never left home; it reveals the blemishes that scream to be treated.

Lester stood exposed on the train as it traversed the globe at impossible speed. The details of the world outside the train blurred into a constant stream of diverse colors that shifted through the spectrum too quickly for any one color in particular to be noticed. He saw it all. When he looked away from the stream, he saw Draven waiting to ask more questions, ready to point out his own colors. To Lester, outside of time, the speed of the train had no effect. It was not a blur of colors to him, but a still-life painting of misery interrupted by the occasional mistake, the seldom noticed instance of a smile here, a celebration there, a moment of rest somewhere in between.

There was no mercy for him as the train pressed on and made its countless stops, and Lester's odd, unlikely guide had fallen into a well-rehearsed silence, one that isolated him as he walked through hospitals and along city streets, wandered upon mountainsides and through building after building where it became clear that the world never slept and was never alone with silence. Everywhere, even while frozen and void of the passing of time, the world was screaming. Lester nearly shielded his ears from the noiseless shouts, cries, and whispers that would otherwise have gone unheard.

The apathetic faces of the women being herded into brothels and hotel rooms in Islamabad, Kiev, Kuala Lumpur, and Bangkok screamed for rescue. The clenched jaws of the men digging snakes out of the side of a mountain in North Korea shouted for food. The battered bodies of the young boys and women in parking lots and shadowed parks pleaded for justice. They all thrust the broken vibrations of their hearts into walls behind their closed lips, so their cries would never be heard, never be known. But Lester, Lester became their recording device, their answering machine to the world that was never home, and burned into his mind were their faces, their scars. Their tears.

He stood in the no-longer-elusive silence as the train came to an ominously slow stop. The greens and dark blues outside had faded into the tail of the still wind so that he had been staring into a steady stream of sand-colored browns and sunburned blue sky until the blur came into focus. Outside was a broken asphalt road that curved and stretched into a flat, shortened horizon of light brown silt and dull green shrubs. Before he could step onto that broken road, the silence was finally broken.

"Last stop."

He shifted to his right so that he could fully see Draven. His guide was characteristically stoic, standing in his typical fashion with both hands in pockets, his head slightly tilted back.

"Are you ready?"

Lester did not bother to respond. He simply took a deep breath as he stared with indifference at the dreadlocked stranger, who had taken him from his home—from his peaceful, little chaotic world—and forced him to stare into monsters ten time worse than the ones that had kept him awake at night as a child. Wanting nothing to do with him but no longer really caring, Lester turned without a sound and left the train.

He stood on dull, light gray asphalt, staring into a dirt field that looked as if it had never been inhabited by house or crop. The train had pulled up to the opposite side of the road, so Lester was now standing out in the open on the short stretch of road that passed a dark brown, pyramid-like structure in the field to his left and opposite from where he stood. As he became aware of the structure, Lester turned toward it to get a full view, instantly awed by its presence. It towered at least a hundred feet up and stretched at least twice that in length. Leading to the top was a long, tier-stepped stairway of well-preserved brick wide enough for several people to walk up side-by-side. Though the structure resembled a pyramid, the top was flat and appeared to have eroded much at its highest peak.

He was about to walk in that direction when he felt a pull, some unseen force turning first his head, then shoulders, and finally his entire body until his back was to the structure. Small shrubs and trees formed lines to the left and right of the road in the distance, and there were scattered homes the same color as the sandy fields. All of those things became the background for the centerpiece of the four vehicles on the road in front of him. He became conscious of the silence again as he took a single, stuttered step forward. The scraping of his shoe on the road was like the amplified sound of a match being dragged across the edge of a box and, suddenly, instantly sucking in oxygen and spitting out a spark and a flame. He froze, more incapable of moving than the time-locked scene he now stood a part of.

The vehicles were familiar and less than a hundred feet away. Their sand-colored, matte paint would have blended with the background if not for the dusty gray road and sparse, dull green vegetation behind and beside them. He had begun walking toward them without realizing it and quickened his pace as details became clearer. Each of the vehicles had a square front with a heavy gate bumper and a plate armored turret that housed a man behind a mounted machine gun. He ran.

He had not run far before he came to a stop, still well-short of the vehicles. His heart was beating so quickly that he worried it would explode from his chest, and he was suddenly fighting to breathe; but he knew that it was not from running a meager fifty feet. The slender man in body armor and helmet in the turret of the first vehicle was standing up and turned around. His arms were over his head, captured while waving to the vehicles behind him.

Lester took a slow step forward, but when he was about to set his foot down, he noticed that the ground was higher beneath his foot. He held his leg up and looked down. There, at his feet, was a mound of dirt filling a large hole in the road. Plastic yellow caps were sticking out of the dirt, but he could not tell what sort of caps they were. They were flat at the very top and then angled diagonally to the edges smoothly. A thin, single strand of black wire was protruding from the dirt and lying across the road. He followed it with his head and eyes as far as he could, but it disappeared into the field beyond the road. He gasped and stumbled backwards several clumsy steps until he fell on the ground.

"They're mortar rounds," Draven said from behind him. Lester nearly fainted when the unexpected voice broke the deathly quiet. He quickly got to his feet so that he could look at Draven. His hands were folded instead of in their usual pants pocket placement.

"But they spotted them in the road." Lester pointed toward the vehicles. "Look, the gunner is signaling the rest of the patrol." He let his arm lower gradually as he finished his thought. "So, they're gonna be okay, right?"

Draven gave no reaction at first, which caused Lester to turn about nervously, throwing his hands up in the air several times. "Right?" He finally shouted when Draven had not said anything. Then he forced himself to stand still and wait.

Draven lifted his head in a slight nod, indicating the patrol of humvees behind Lester. "Go."

"I'm not going over there. They're gonna be okay, right?"

Another nod. "Go."

Lester stomped with one foot. "I am not going over there. I refuse to play your stupid game anymore!"

Draven was practically a mannequin. He made no motion to respond, only stared stoically at Lester.

Lester clenched his fists and breathed hard through his nose. "No." He clenched his teeth so hard that it hurt. "No."

Draven nodded again. "Go."

Lester closed his eyes and seethed, hissing his angry breaths through his teeth and clenching his fists. Close. Open. Breathe. Close.

Open. Breathe. He opened his eyes and was about to tell Draven exactly what he thought of him, but his guide was not there. Neither was the train. They had both vanished. He stood alone on the road in the longest, deepest, and most profound silence of his life.

And then there was the scraping of his shoes as he turned in circles. Somehow, he knew not to shout, not to call out for Draven. He was gone. As sure as he had appeared suddenly, he had disappeared without warning. The train, he thought, must have been attached to his guide, a strange connection with his otherworldly clerical power. Lester felt a fleeting flutter of relief as he realized he was not going to look into those finger-pointing eyes again or ride the hover-train across the imaginary rails into his own death-collage of madness.

But there were the vehicles to think about. He turned and squared his body with the first Humvee. Unable to move, he looked back over his shoulder at the massive structure which, in that instant, was no longer unfamiliar. He mentally roamed his memory of pictures Dillon had sent him. Pictures of Dillon smiling with Iraqi children, men, and women. Pictures of Dillon standing in front of bridges, monuments, and historical lands that all seemed so impressive to Lester. But most impressive to him of all the pictures saved in his emails and desktop folder was the structure Dillon had told him was called the Ziggurat of Dur-Kurigalzu. The ziggurat that Dillon patrolled past every day.

He turned his head slowly back to the Humvees, then down and to the side where the mortar rounds still barely protruded from the ground, attached to the wire. He walked at first, then jogged, then ran as fast as his legs could take him, shouting Dillon's name as he covered the distance to the Humvee in great strides. The faces of the crew inside the vehicle came into focus, and he saw that there were names on the flat windshields of them. The driver's side had the name and rank of the driver Dillon had told him about: PFC Johnson. The passenger side windshield read: SSG Sharp.

"Dillon!"

He was so focused on the name and rank of his brother, followed by the face of his sibling appearing in the window that he ran into the front bumper of the Humvee. He grunted as his next breath was sucked away from him prematurely, but he was scrambling around the front of the vehicle hand over hand from the bumper to the hood to the passenger door. The window on the door was small and square, and it protruded out in such a way that the top was angled out farther than the bottom. Lester hunched down, so that he could look into the narrow window, and shouted his brother's name.

Dillon was leaning forward in the seat. One hand was stretched out so that the gloved fingertips of his right hand were nearly pressed against the inside of the windshield. His left hand was braced palm flat into a computer screen that had a satellite image of the place they were standing. The computer screen was cased in thick, green plastic, and it was in front of a stack of radios and other equipment. Most of it was out of Lester's view, blocked by Dillon's vest and helmet, but Lester only noticed any of it in passing. He was intent on Dillon's face. He wanted the panicked look to change, wanted Dillon to turn and acknowledge him. He pounded his fists into the window and shouted Dillon's name several times, but the mannequins inside the Humvee were unresponsive.

Lester growled and spun away from the Humvee. Fists clenched at his sides, head stretched to the sky, he yelled as loud as he could. It was a desperate cry, a primal scream born from frustration. He knew, had known since he saw the name on the vehicle, that there was no changing the circumstances. Now he was trapped there. He had no idea how much longer the glimpse would last, but he knew that he did not have the strength to stand by and watch his brother run over the trap in the road and be blown up. He leaned back and yelled again, straining through it until his body forced him to stop in a fit of coughing. Chest heaving, tears streaming down his face, he turned and then yanked on the door handle of the Humvee.

Nothing.

He pulled again, harder this time. He yelled Dillon's name and "no" in protest, again and again while repeatedly yanking on the door handle—to no avail. His mind went back to the Skype call a week prior, to the conversation about Dillon and his soldiers being ordered to lock the doors while out on patrols and how dangerous that was because they were often required to get out of their vehicles quickly. Lester remembered his words as well; he had told Dillon that he wanted him to lock the doors to keep out the people that wanted to hurt him. None of that mattered to him in that moment. He wanted to get to his brother, to pull him to safety. This was the last stop. If Draven was gone, the glimpse could end soon. He had the brief thought that he would pull the other men out, too, unless the glimpse ended too soon.

But he had to get Dillon. He pounded and yelled until he was too tired and his arms and fists were too bruised to continue. He put his forehead against the window and pounded to the sides of his head one last, weak time. He hated the sound of his own sobbing against the echoing silence, for it echoed the words of his guide like a record player stuck on repeat of the same chord. He had already forgotten the driver's name, and it occurred to him that he had not thought of his parents once. Each sob became a chip in the silence, a gash in his conscious that became a mental storage unit filled with a dead man in a prison, an elderly couple leaning on one another late into the night, a dead mother beside her newborn baby and downwind of her attacker, a beheaded pastor beneath his lynched wife, pre-adolescent sex victims, and starving prostitutes.

His body shook beyond his control with the onset of the agonizing flow of tears he could not stem. "Why?" he asked through sobbing, numb lips. "Why did You make me see these things?" He heard his voice echoing into the metal of the Humvee and the road at his feet. There was a hollowness to it that seemed to be born of something more than a simple echo. He closed his eyes and pleaded, hoping he was being heard.

"Why won't You help them? Why show me this if there's no way to save them?" He hit the door with his fists again, even weaker this time. "How can You just sit by and let this happen to my brother? To all of those people?"

A voice behind him spoke. "How can *you*?"

Lester gasped and turned around quickly. There, standing on the lawn of Lester's house in the dark of night, was Draven.

Chapter 11

GRAVITY

GRAVITY IS INESCAPABLE. IT IS in all things and will not be ignored. Neither is it merciful or selective. It carries its rule like a crown and forces all of its subjects—no matter how high or seemingly untouchable—to eventually come down. From a child's ball tossed playfully into the air to the preacher lording over his congregation, everything must eventually submit to gravity. It is a force stronger than any amount of propulsion or pride.

Lester felt that force crushing him, bearing down on him as he stared through watery eyes in the darkness at his guide. He wanted nothing more than to charge the man and rip the dreadlocks from his scalp, to punch the grim and flat smile from his face; but he was sinking, shrinking down and away. He vaguely registered that his back had suddenly hit something hard, knew but could not believe that it was the outside wall of his house. Then he was sitting on the ground, cold and afraid, and he still felt the powerful hands of gravity trying to force him deeper. His strength had failed him both mentally and physically.

"It can't be real," he whispered. "It can't be real." He could not focus his sight on any particular spot because he felt like he was spinning; so his head and eyes shifted from his feet to Draven, then the sky with its cryptically clear silver moon, and finally back to the overgrown lawn before the nauseating cycle began again. Strong, intrusive hands gripped the sides of his head, and he felt and smelled the sweet warmth of fresh breath upon his face. The spinning stopped, and he looked into shining blue eyes in a dark face. Their light was not a reflection of the moon; theirs was an impossible, enchanting glow that pulled Lester into their depths.

"Sit up." Draven's voice was firm and soothing. "And for once, listen."

"My brother," Lester said and nearly choked on the words.

A shake of his head. "Listen!"

"How can you let that happen to my brother?" Lester sniffled. "All those people. Why?"

Draven forced him to his feet, pulling on him with strength that defied the man's skinny frame. Lester felt his back being pushed against the wall of the house, and a strong hand was on his chest. "Shut up, and listen."

"No." Lester forced his sobs back down and sobered himself. He looked directly into Draven's face with the last ounce of confidence he could muster. "I'm not shutting up, and I'm not listening. I want answers." He pushed Draven away from himself violently, and his guide stumbled backwards.

Draven straightened and smoothed his shirt. "Oh, you want answers?"

Lester nodded. "And I'm not doing anything else you say until I get them."

Draven laughed. "You wanna know how I can stand by and let all those things happen, Lester? Is that what you want to know?"

He nodded again.

"You know, it's funny, man, because I want to know the same thing about you." He pointed at Lester. "You and everyone like you that don't have a reason not to. Tell me why you just live your life, knowing all that mess is going on in the world, and you do nothing. You tell me."

Lester snorted. "Knowing it?" He touched a finger to his chest. "How am I supposed to know that all of that is going on? I'd never seen any of it until tonight."

"See, man?" Draven sighed and shook his head. "That's where you're wrong. Man, you've seen all of it a thousand times. It's on the news every day. You see the ads up in the stores, the post office, all over the place for missing kids. You read about it when you're scrolling through everything else on your phone. You know you used to read those magazines you just leave lying around for months and then throw away on cleaning day. Oh, you've seen it. You're just too stuck on *you* to care—too stuck on what you want and how you think the world works to help a guy that comes into your shop asking for food."

Lester waved his hands in front of his face. "Nice speech, but you don't know as much as you think."

"And you don't know anything." Draven shrugged. "You just saw it all with your own eyes, and it's like I said before: you only care about what affects you." He shook his head. "Come on, man, what are you thinking about right now?"

"What any sane person would be thinking about." Lester nearly shouted. "My brother's about to drive over a bomb and die, and there's nothing I can do about it. As soon as this glimpse or whatever is over, I won't have a brother anymore."

Draven put his hands back in his pockets and made a grunting noise through his nose. "Who said he was going to die?"

Lester's jaw dropped and his mouth fell open. "What?"

"You heard me."

"So, he's going to live?" Lester felt his heart beating faster.

Draven shrugged. "I don't know, Lester. It's not for me to know, or you, but what makes you say there's nothing you can do?"

Lester shook his head. "I don't understand."

"That's because you don't listen. None of you do. Seven billion people talking all at once. Only a few saying anything worth hearing, and no one paying attention because you won't just stop. You've got your jobs and your devices, your games, your habits and hobbies, and you constantly have to be busy and entertained. And every last one of you has someone right down the street that needs your help. I've been watching it for thousands of years; and no matter how much the hairstyles and the houses change, you all stay exactly the same."

"Did you just say thousands of years?" Lester cocked his head to the side.

Draven laughed. "Still don't get it, huh?"

Lester held his arms out wide. "Get what? What do you want from me?"

Draven shook his head. "I'm just your guide, Lester, and the tour is over. It's never been about what *I* want."

"Fine, then what does your *Boss* want from me?" He paced a few steps back and forth, then stopped and threw his hands up again. "He sends me around the world to look at a bunch of helpless people that are beyond saving, and for what? So I can feel guilty? Well, mission accomplished. I feel guilty. It's horrible that all of those things are happening, but what can I do? And what about my brother? Does your Boss not care about the fact that I'm literally one second away from losing my brother?"

"Who said they're beyond saving?" Draven's face was stoic. His stance was casual.

"You're telling me the dead mother and her baby can be saved?"

"No." Draven shook his head. "But there's always going to be a mother and a baby like them. Just like all the rest of the people you saw. The actors change, man, but the script stays the same." He shrugged. "And what makes you say there's nothing you can do?"

Lester leaned back against the wall of the house and looked at his feet. "What can I possibly do?"

"Like I said, I'm just your guide, and the tour is over."

"I thought a guide was supposed to give advice."

"Who says I haven't?"

Lester did not respond. He stared at his shoes and the ground. He thought of all the people and places he had seen. His mind drifted, while his eyes stayed fixed, drifted across town, into the city, across an ocean, onto a dry field, into cold mountains, next to an ancient temple, and, finally, beside an armored vehicle. He stared into the dirty window, into the wide, terrified eyes of his brother. He wanted his mind to stay in that moment, to stay in that place where Dillon was close, but he knew his mind would come back to the ground beneath his shoes.

He whispered through the window, whispered his love and a tearful goodbye, and then he lifted his mind's eye to the bright, somehow peaceful sky and whispered to it, through it, and beyond. He whispered to the Throne he once believed was there but could no longer see, pleaded despite his fears for Dillon and the rest of his patrol to be spared. He whispered for two men on a mountainside, digging for snakes to find food. He whispered for young girls and boys and women in cities around the world to make it home. He whispered for a tiny congregation on the Horn of Africa to endure and find hope in the midst of hopelessness. He whispered and whispered until he felt a cool breeze carrying his whispers in its hands, not from his mind's eye, but beyond his shoes and into the darkness of night to the deeper dark and beyond, where he hoped there was still enough light shining to make a whisper a song.

He looked up, and he was alone. A familiar voice drifted with the breeze of unfrozen time.

"I'll be watching, Lester."

Weighted down by grief and unwelcome resolve, Lester coaxed gravity into helping him up the steps and into the house.

Chapter 12

INTO THE LIGHT

LIGHT IS THE ONLY NATURAL repellant to darkness. Man, afraid of what may or may not be residing in the dark, clings to any form of light available, as if the inception of light will dispel mythical creatures or epically guilt-saturated pasts, which lie in wait. Often, it is not the fear of a *thing* or someone that cripples a person, but the fear of the self that can only be found in the solitude and loneliness of darkness. There, void of distractions and sounds, sharpened and prepared, are the stinging secrets never told and the thorns of regret. And so, nervous fingers fumble through the heaviness of pitch blackness to find switches and usher in unnatural light, which is no more capable of dispelling the monsters of an unrepentant mind than human vices.

Lester was desperate for light as he entered the house and had violently slapped upward the switch on the wall to his left before ever closing the door. Instant, false comfort flooded the room from ceiling to floor and washed over him with imaginary warmth. He fell against the door and held himself up by the doorknob, tucking his face into his shoulder and against the cold wood grain. There was no reason to hold back, so he let himself cry, let himself grieve; but now that he was not just mourning his brother, he could hardly bear the violent convulsions of his body and the swirling collage of countless lives hanging in the balance as he shed tear upon salty tear.

With his eyes closed, not even the sense of comfort found in the cheap, incandescent light bulbs could help him. Lester was standing in his living room and racing around the world at dizzying speed, so dizzying that he fell and hit his face on the unfairly warm floor. It was somehow smooth and comforting, and he curled into it like an infant in a bassinet; but he could not squeeze his legs and arms in tight enough. He could not groan loudly enough or scream with enough agony to make it all go away. He gave up on the futile effort to silence the screams that had made their way through the silence of cities, mountains, deserts, and oceans, and crawled through the house. On hands and knees, with water-flooded eyes misleading and guiding him, he made his way to the bedroom.

Desperate, he pushed himself to his feet, using the door jamb of the bedroom for balance, and ran across the room to his dresser. A picture of him and Dillon in front of the coffee shop next to the park brought another groan and more tears, but he was devoted to his mind's orders to his fingers. Trembling hands grasped brass handles and yanked a drawer open. He gingerly pulled stacks of various colored shirts up and out of his way at first, then growled and yanked the drawer off of the rails and out of the dresser. It fell with him to the thick carpet with a dull thud, and clothes spilled out. Lester tore through them with abandon, tossing some to the side, throwing others over his shoulders, crying through it all and blinking away streams of tears that never seemed to end. Finally, when he thought that he would never get to the source of his query, he found the shirt he was looking for.

He grabbed a red shirt by the shoulders and held it up. The words in white on the front—THE WATCHMEN—stood out in stark contrast, even in the dim light that had seeped through from the living room. He pulled the words toward himself and buried his face in the shirt, and he cried again, sobbing with no shame. He heard his own, muffled voice repeating: "Forgive me, forgive me."

A knock at the door pulled him away, and he sat up straight with a gasp. He lowered the shirt to his lap and looked over to the red LED display of his alarm clock. It was five minutes past midnight. He was about to fall into another fit of sobs when the knock was repeated, louder this time. Lester slowly got to his feet, clutching the shirt in one hand, and then walked out of the bedroom hesitantly. As he entered the living room again, he heard a voice on the other side of the door calling out, muffled but decidedly real.

"Hello?"

Lester cleared the short distance and slowly turned the doorknob, then pulled the door back cautiously. It was his neighbor, the man whom he had performed CPR on. He was standing on the other side of the door on Lester's steps with a grim expression, eyes down, and somewhat swaying. Lester froze momentarily, utterly shocked that the man was alive, much less standing at his door.

"Sorry to bother you so late," his neighbor said, looking up. "Name's Wayne. We met one time when our mail got mixed up. At least, I think that's what happened."

Shakily, Lester responded. "I . . . um . . . yeah. I remember."

"Yes sir," Wayne said with a slight nod. "Well, I um . . . what am I doing?"

"It's alright, Wayne," Lester interrupted. "What can I do for you?"

Wayne took a deep breath, a long and heavy breath that moved his chest and shoulders up and down. "I don't know anybody, and, um, I guess you could say I'm just having a real bad night. I saw your light come on a couple minutes ago."

Lester stood, holding the door close to his face, staring out into the night at the man he had tried to save, and the words Draven had spoken to him on the lawn came to his mind: "Who said they were beyond saving?"

He hesitated, gripping the shirt in his hand, and then he nodded. "You wanna come in, Wayne?" The man looked up, eyes wide. "I think my coffee's just about burnt, but I could put on a fresh pot." He held back tears and a lump in his throat that was threatening to burst out. "You look like you could use a cup."

Wayne blinked rapidly, then reached up and wiped his face as quickly as he could. "Yes, sir. I believe a good cup of coffee'd do me good." Lester stepped back and to the side, opening the door wide enough for his neighbor to enter. Wayne walked in timidly, giving Lester a nod.

Lester held out his hand. "I'm Lester."

Wayne looked down at the extended hand, visibly trying to keep himself from swooning, and then took it in his own. They shook, and then Lester led him to a seat, talking to him as they walked.

* * * * *

After he had made coffee and brought a cup for himself, he handed another to his guest before taking his own seat across from him.

Wayne thanked him and took a few, tiny sips. "That's good, Lester. I sure appreciate it."

"My pleasure."

Wayne nodded his head toward the back of the house. "I noticed when I walked up, that your car's not in the driveway. Is it in the shop or something?"

Lester laughed. For the first time that he could remember, Lester laughed.

FATE
OF THE
REDEEMED

CHAD PETTIT

COMING SOON
FATE OF THE REDEEMED

Chapter 1

THE WATCHER STOOD SILENTLY, ENSHROUDED by the ageless camouflage that is the Realm of the Watchers. Here is the place of no place, a tangible reality only to the immortal, supernatural players on a timeless battlefield for the souls of mankind. This is where bumps in the nights are born, where unanticipated tempests of raging lightning and rain lash out on a fallen earth as the elemental warriors dance their cosmic dance of undying death.

The watcher smiled. Comfortably. Peacefully. Transitioning from his human form of dark skin and long dreadlocks, he kept his immortal gaze fixed on the quiet house, the house he had just left, where a newly-reformed soul now comforted a man snatched from the claws of death. A single light in the living room of the house remained on—its faint yellow glow beaming through the night like a beacon atop a lone lighthouse that faithfully guides lost ships to its reassuring shores.

He let out a sigh, letting down his guard to complete the transition. Dark brown, sinewy arms began to turn into bulkier but still slender arms that blended into the shades of myriad colors surrounding him. He shifted his attention to this, enjoying the spell of the ever-changing skin tones. Dark green and shadow, like the grass at his feet. Yellow and glowing, like the light from the house. He turned his hand so the palm was facing him and wiggled his fingers in order to watch them rapidly change between the mixtures of color and light.

His pleasure at the sight was intense but unmatched by the elation of the night's victory. Centuries behind this invisible curtain, decade after decade watching the unaware immortals go through their endless loop of birth and death, killing and being killed, starving and warring. Year after year, like seconds to Draven, the watcher for so long, but tonight it had been different. He had been allowed to go to one of them, to show his power in the presence of an immortal and be a part of the reclamation of a soul.

He looked up from his transparent hand to the house. A part of him wanted to go to Lester, to listen to him as he spoke to Wayne, the man whom Lester had saved with what he had then believed to be pointless, futile life-saving measures. He wanted to, but he would not. Could not. He saw that the light was out. They had fallen asleep, and Draven's chance to experience humanity was over. In the next moment, his peace ended more abruptly than the light had gone out.

He heard the vacuum of wind created by the hit before he felt it, felt its searing bite before he saw the burst of light it caused as the fist of smoldering electricity crashed into his transitioning temple. He was on the ground then, his half-mortal, half-immortal head slamming into the dirt with another burst of white light. Powerful hands pulled him to his right and then onto his back. He stared through a haze of clear black into the blue, lightning colored eyes of a dark, towering figure.

Morane.

He was head and shoulders taller than Draven, half a foot wider, and harnessed the power of lightning, which was evident by the electricity dancing along his body and sparking at the end of his enormous fingertips. The haze in Draven's vision cleared enough for him to make out the details of the demon's wide, inhuman face. A watcher can see through the darkest abyss, so Draven had no difficulty seeing clearly that this was, indeed, his nemesis, even though the oily black skin of the demon blended perfectly into the moonless night. He smiled with a hiss, revealing razor sharp teeth that were so brilliantly white they could stand in as lights in a cave. Their glow temporarily drowned out Morane's face.

"Quite a show, Draven," Morane said in a snarling, guttural voice. "A pity you won't be able to see the unhappy ending."

Draven clenched his teeth and tried to get to his feet. He was weakened by the blow, so he would not be able to transition into his true form without getting away from the demon. The giant, clawed hand grabbing him by the throat made it clear that it was not going to happen. He swung his arms, saw them pass through Morane's thick, black hide and mentally berated himself for taking so long to transform. In their transitive state, his arms were useless on both planes.

"Caught off guard, watcher?" Morane laughed and slammed his head into Draven's. The force of the demon's square head cracking into his forehead nearly made Draven black out, but he didn't have time to assess the damage or pain because a series of right hand punches pummeled into his face in rapid succession. He swooned, feeling his throat nearly collapsing under the pressure of Morane's other hand, and then he was on the ground again. He felt the impact as if in a distant tunnel, as if the force of the impact was delayed, and he realized he was losing consciousness.

"You won't win, Morane," he said through his partly-crushed throat, his words a raspy whisper. The words sounded pathetic, tiny and echoing from the far end of a long tunnel.

Morane picked him up by the chest and legs, lifted him high, and then slammed him onto the ground. Draven heard his breath blast out in a gust with a groan that may have been his. He felt something splatter on his face, something cold and wet. His blood. Again he was lifted, again he was slammed down. More blood sprayed. More air blasted out. He could no longer breathe, but a distant memory of something important called to him, willed him to stand. He turned his head, caught a glimpse of a dark house on a pleasant lawn at night. He wondered whose home it was, and then his jaw was hit from one side, and the other slammed into the ground with a sickening crack.

The rebound of the hit forced his eyes skyward. Lightning surged above him, then into him. His body lifted involuntarily with a wicked jolt. He clenched his teeth and grimaced in pain. The lightning stopped, and he collapsed. He registered a thousand nerve endings, all firing at once, and he wondered if they were his. It was all so distant. He heard a voice above him, telling him someone named Lester would never survive what was coming. He wondered who Lester was, wondered who he was. Another bolt of lightning. This time there was no strength in him to clench his teeth or grimace. His body did what the lightning told it to do, collapsed when the lightning left and gave it permission.

He was in the air then, up at first, then soaring. Wind in his ears. Through the hazy black cloud, he saw the night fade to day, and the temperature changed. He felt something on his back, hard at first and then he was sliding through whatever it was. Above him, there was a blackened sun and a sky that should have been bright. It faded to onyx as he slipped into a sleep like none he had known before.

* * * * *

Finished with his work, the demon, Morane, turned to face the house as he allowed his lightning to return to his core where it would lie dormant until he needed it again. He grinned, feeling his sharp teeth fold over his thin, bottom lip. Bringing his hands up toward his face, he grasped his right wrist in his left hand and rubbed it. The burning sensation caused by a century in chains was nearly unbearable, but he relished in the victory over the one who had put him in them all those years ago.

Years. He scoffed audibly. A century. The blink of an eye to the mighty Morane, lieutenant to Lucifer himself. He had waited patiently in the depths of Hades, ticking the years like seconds on a clock while he plotted his revenge. This was their way. He had lost to Draven before. The puny watcher was nothing compared to Morane in open combat, but the tiny warrior had prowess and cunning. Morane marvelled that Draven had been so easily caught off his guard. Apparently, the soft-hearted angel had been so engrossed in the reformation of this mortal that he had forgotten the dangers lurking all about him.

Morane smiled again. How fortunate for him it all was. He suffered none of Draven's weaknesses. In fact, he allowed none of the hindrances that so often crippled those of the host still loyal to Jehovah. Obedience, loyalty, compassion; these were the marks of a fool and had no place on the battlefield of true warriors. Among titans, mercy meant death. Of course, Morane knew that Draven was not dead, and he would have to go and check on him soon so that he could further cripple him, but he had time for that later.

"Time for you now, Lester," he said.

Yes. Time to show Lester that his choice to forsake his ways and follow Jehovah was a mistake. Not just a mistake: suicide. Lester just didn't realize it. Yet.

Morane laughed to himself. "Enjoy your rest, Lester," he said to himself. "Tomorrow, your life is in the hands of Morane."

He vanished.

* * * * *

Voices.

Someone was shouting. No, many voices. Many men, all shouting, and the voices were coming closer. He heard them, tried to discern the words. They escaped him for a moment, but then his mind cycled through the languages to translate the words. He wondered how he was able to do that, but the translation clicked, and the urgency of the words became clear.

Sorcerer. The voices were shouting "sorcerer," and they were getting closer. He scrambled to his feet, swooned, and fell to his knees. A cough violently forced its way out of his throat, and blood splattered onto the sand.

Sand?

It was daylight. Was it supposed to be daylight? Was there supposed to be sand here? Where was here? He saw a flash of darkness in his mind, thought he remembered a small house on a perfect lawn, but that could not be right. He was on his knees in the sand. A desert. There were no lawns here, wherever here was.

The voices were close. He lifted his right arm to shield his eyes from the glaring sun, but his arm wasn't there. At least, it didn't appear to be there. The sun shone through it, and he saw the faint, clear silhouette of a sinewy arm. He lowered his head and lifted his left arm. Both hands were in front of his face as he looked down. Dark skin began to appear, chasing the transparent skin away. He let out a gasp and fell to his back. The sand was hot and burned his skin, so he got to his feet again.

Pain wracked his body. Forcing his chin as close to his chest as he could so that he could inspect himself, he saw that he was covered in scorch marks. His clothes were shredded. Gingerly, he reached up and touched his cheek bone. It was swollen and felt like it was on fire. His fingertips were covered in blood when he pulled his hand away. One eye, he realized, was nearly swollen shut, but he saw the men who owned the voices then. Saw them past the blood on his hand; saw them through one eye that threatened to shut for good if he did not blink away the stinging tears caused by the sun's relentless rays.

He did blink, squeezing his eyes tightly shut before opening them. The men were closer when he opened his eye again, and he saw rifles in their hands. Their faces were wrapped in black cloths that were also wrapped around their heads and necks. Only their eyes were showing, and he was amazed that he could see this because they were still several hundred feet away. How could he see so far and hear them so clearly? A building burned behind them, and he saw a body hanging from a tree next to the building. He thought it was familiar, thought he was supposed to recognize it.

Whimpering.

His head ticked in the direction of the sound. Quiet, muffled, but the sound was definitely someone whimpering. He rolled onto his hands and knees and crawled quickly toward the sound. It was feminine and young. A girl. He did not know how he knew, but he knew. He located the sound, depended on his ears to guide him and kept his good eye shut against the sting of the sunlight. Not far from where he had been was a thicket of brush. He crawled around it and found a girl huddled there, lying on the ground with her arms clutched about her head. She was young. Five, he knew, but did not know how he knew.

Yara. Her name was Yara, but he did not know how he knew. He crawled to her and reached out. She moved her arms from her head quickly and turned her face so that she was looking directly at him. She screamed, and he crawled back in panic. The voices behind him were very loud now, and shots from the rifles were fired into the air. Yara jumped to her feet. He stood and went to her as more shots were fired into the air, except, they were not fired into the air. Bullets stung his back and legs, went through his not-quite-dark, not-quite-sinewy arms. The girl screamed. Yara screamed. Her head went back and her mouth released a cry of agony.

He did not think; he acted, but he did not know why he did what he did next. He reached his not-quite-solid hand into her very-much-solid shoulder where the bullet had gone in and pulled it out. He then moved his body in front of hers and let the bullet fall from his fingers as he fell on top of her. The girl vanished. Yara disappeared, and he fell to the sand with a grunt. Now disoriented even more than before, he laid there for a moment until he heard the voices behind him.

He stood, faced the men. Faced the voices. Bullets fell out of his back as he fell to his knees. How? He did not know. They said "sorcerer" again. They were calling *him* a sorcerer, he realized. A rifle struck his solid face, and he had no strength to block it with his now-solid arm. He saw the building in the distance burning as he fell to the ground and wondered why he knew it was a church. He wondered where the girl had gone. Where Yara had gone.

His face hit the ground, and he knew only darkness.

DID YOU ENJOY THIS BOOK?

Here are some ways to share it with others!

Please consider leaving us a review on Amazon, Goodreads, Barnes and Noble, or christianbook.com {or wherever!}.

Write a review on your blog.

Share or mention the book on your social media using the hashtag #FateoftheWatchman.

Let us know personally on Twitter or Facebook by tagging us at @AmbassadorIntl.

On Instagram? Post a picture and tag us at @chad_pettit_ and @AmbassadorIntl – we love seeing real life pictures of our books!

Let others know by sharing this message: "I enjoyed #FateoftheWatchman by Chad Pettit and @AmbassadorIntl."

Most importantly, recommend this book to your friends, family, coworkers, book club, etc.

Your support for Chad Pettit and Ambassador International is most appreciated.

Before time froze, angels and demons battled for a man's soul.

Hidden among the rooftops of a dark city, the archangel, Orac watches as a lone vehicle travels into the night. Armed with his fiery sword and orders to protect the driver of the vehicle at all costs, Orac takes flight. He seizes on the element of surprise to defeat the demon, Talnuc, but soon discovers that the demon is not alone...

An angel with amnesia. A demon with a vendetta. The man caught in their crossfire.

Lester Sharp has been given a second chance to live a life of compassion, but his decision to follow God will be tested when his estranged father calls to tell him his brother has been killed in combat. A demon unleashes a series of attacks on him, and someone he thought was lost to his past emerges.

Lester is guarded by the angel, Draven, but when Morane catches the watcher off his guard, Draven loses his memory and finds himself being held prisoner in a remote Somali village. His only ally is Ibrahim, a man who finds out his son has been murdered by extremists when his granddaughter appears out of nowhere and somehow possesses supernatural powers.

As Morane's fury is unleashed, time is running out for Lester, and Draven's fate is in the hands of a man whose faith is being pushed to the limit.

For more information about
Chad Pettit
&
Fate of the Watchman
please visit:

www.chadpettit.net
www.facebook.com/ChadPettit.Writer
@pettit_chad
www.instagram.com/pettit_chad

For more information about
AMBASSADOR INTERNATIONAL
please visit:

www.ambassador-international.com
@AmbassadorIntl
www.facebook.com/AmbassadorIntl

*If you enjoyed this book, please consider leaving us a review on
Amazon, Goodreads, or our website.*